It suddenly hit me this morning ~~how~~ ~~unfathom-~~ **able it is that I'm going to b**~~... ~~ ~~... says not~~ to worry, that I ~~will~~ ~~...~~ ~~...~~ vely, but will sometimes ~~...~~ ~~...~~ inten- tions. Some bes~~...~~ ~~...~~ me in many ways that ~~...~~ ~~...~~rstands what I'm going ~~...~~ ~~...~~ for maternity bras on Tuesday ~~...~~ ~~...~~dy substantial breasts are swelling past the point of reason; sore and tingling every day now, and she teased me endlessly about my new, darkly shaded nipples. . . .

Times like this with Calista remind me just how much I cherish our friendship. I adore your daddy, but there is something between women that men can never match. Even though it's hard for the two of us to find time for the careful attention our friendship deserves, I believe that when we put the energy in, something amazing comes back to us. Sometimes I long for the time when a woman's job consisted of gathering daily with the women in her life: sewing, cooking, gardening, watching each other's children, spending their days talking and laughing and healing each other's wounds. The quilting way of life, Nana called it. "It's not the act of making a quilt that really matters," she'd say. "It's the time women used to have together. They were each other's strength."

"Heart-wrenching and life-affirming and hard to
put down."
—Jean Hegland, author of *Into the Forest*

the KIND *of* LOVE

THAT SAVES YOU

AMY YURK

Bantam Books

NEW YORK TORONTO LONDON

SYDNEY AUCKLAND

This edition contains the complete text
of the original hardcover edition.
NOT ONE WORD HAS BEEN OMITTED.

THE KIND OF LOVE THAT SAVES YOU
A Bantam Book

PUBLISHING HISTORY
Bantam hardcover edition published May 2000
Bantam mass market edition / June 2001

All rights reserved.
Copyright © 2000 by Amy Yurk.
Cover art copyright © 2000 by Royce M. Becker.

Library of Congress Catalog Card Number: 99-462332
No part of this book may be reproduced or transmitted in any form or
by any means, electronic or mechanical, including photocopying,
recording, or by any information storage and retrieval system, without
permission in writing from the publisher.
For information address: Bantam Books.

If you purchased this book without a cover you should be aware that
this book is stolen property. It was reported as "unsold and
destroyed" to the publisher and neither the author nor the publisher
has received any payment for this "stripped book."

ISBN-13: 978-0-553-58217-8

Published simultaneously in the United States and Canada

Bantam Books are published by Bantam Books, a division of Random
House, Inc. Its trademark, consisting of the words "Bantam Books" and
the portrayal of a rooster, is Registered in U.S. Patent and Trademark
Office and in other countries. Marca Registrada. Bantam Books, 1540
Broadway, New York, New York 10036.

PRINTED IN THE UNITED STATES OF AMERICA

OPM   10 9 8 7 6 5 4 3

For Trinka,

who always believed

ACKNOWLEDGMENTS

For their help in the mystical transformation from manuscript to book, my warmest thanks go out to my agent, Victoria Sanders, for her patience and sharp wit, and to my editor, Christine Brooks, for seeing the story I wanted to tell and gently coaxing it to the page.

To my husband, Eric, for making room for me to take this journey, and to Audra Sipple Spath, for providing invaluable insight during the early stages of this story, I stand before you both, eternally grateful. Thanks also to Lori Waters, for putting a serious shot of mojo in my pen, and to Gabe Travers, for serving as a grand source of baby inspiration.

Lastly, my thanks to you, dear reader, for taking me in your hands: May my words find a home in your heart.

Prologue

I know you are young. I know you think it could never happen to you. We all think it. We shuffle quietly along, expecting life, expecting blossoms and growth and continuance. We look ahead and see nothing but all our dreams coming true. We are dauntless.

But, as I wish someone had told me when I was your age, here is the truth: Every person's journey is touched by loss. At some point in this life, someone will be taken away from you. The place where they were . . . empty. What you hoped might be . . . gone. Grief will reach in and wrap its roots tightly around your heart. You'll believe the pain will end you.

What I know now and so desperately want you to understand is that the grief that comes from losing someone does not have to be an ending. As with most experiences in life, you have a choice. You can either choose to let grief destroy your world or you can open your eyes to a new one: a world where you are wiser, more appreciative of the rarity of life, fully grateful for the precious time we are given.

Granted, this was the hardest lesson I ever had to learn. But I share it with you now because in the end it became the one that counted most . . . the one I'll never let myself forget. . . .

Fall . . .

Your daddy dropped the bomb a few hours ago. The evening news droned softly in the background as we sat on the sofa after dinner, sharing a Corona and sucking on lime wedges. I was in the middle of telling him that Mike and Calista couldn't get a sitter for next Sunday's dinner plans, when he interrupted me. "We're just not ready to have a baby," he said quickly, as though he had been storing up this announcement like a held breath.

His words didn't surprise me. We've been discussing the possibility of getting pregnant since February. Though lately, as the leaves slip into their vibrant shades of autumn fire, I've begun to think that if you are ever going to be conceived, I'll have to take a needle to my diaphragm.

I waited a moment after he spoke, pulled a long swig off the beer, then set it carefully on the coffee table in front of us. He posed expectantly, leaning forward with wide eyes, waiting for me to agree with him. "Huh," I said, folding my hands carefully on my lap. "Well, then. Sounds like you've got it all figured out. But I'm curious, hon. What exactly does 'ready' mean?"

Pressing his lips into a dark line, he crossed his arms over his chest and shot me a frustrated glance. He hates it when I ask him to explain himself; hates it even more when he doesn't have an explanation. "I just don't feel all the way ready, Sarah," he said. "Okay? Isn't that enough?" I shook my head, moved toward him on the couch, and teasingly poked him in the belly. "Nope. It's not." He pushed my hand away and asked, "Why?"

I sighed, flopping back against the worn cushions. "Because, Gavin. Nobody ever feels all the way ready. I think it's more of a process-type thing. You get more ready as you go through it, you know? You learn things. Calista and Mike weren't 'ready' when she got pregnant with Davie, and they're great parents." Your daddy snorted and rolled his eyes, saying, "Yeah, great parents. Nice marriage too. If I have to hear about his emotional distance or her PMS one more time, I'm going to shoot myself." He took a section of lime and shoved it in his mouth, skin side out, covering his teeth. He smiled hugely, crossing his eyes at me. "Very attractive," I said, laughing. "I'm trying to be serious here, all right? We've been married five years. Our relationship is solid, don't you think? You love me forever, right?" He paused, pretending to have to think about his answer, then nodded as he pulled the mangled fruit from his mouth. "Yeah . . . I guess you're a keeper." I swatted him on the arm. "Hey! I mean it. I want you to want this as much as I do." Tears rippled the edges of my words.

Your daddy placed his hand against my cheek, a gesture that generally calms me. "I get what you're saying, Sarah-bara. I want to want it too, but I need to catch up with you, okay?" I sniffed and nodded, wanting to grab him by the shoulders and shake him, screaming, "No, no, it's not okay!" He took the last swig from the bottle, kissed the top of my head, and went to take a shower. I waited until I heard the water start to rumble through the pipes before I went down the hall and into the closet of space that serves as my office. Messy towers of press releases and promotional CDs littered my desk; I had to dig through a couple of layers before I found the cordless phone. I called your Auntie Calista.

She was in the middle of getting Davie into his pajamas, but when she heard the tremor in my voice, she passed the baby off to Mike and told me she'd go into their bedroom before we continued our conversation. I pictured her settling back into the fluffy pillows on their bed, phone tucked between her ear and shoulder. By this time of night, she would be in her usual evening uniform: gray sweat suit and white socks, her thick black hair pulled back in a tight ponytail. Her face would be shiny and clean, moisturizer applied evenly. Calista has always prided herself on an efficient beauty routine, while I'm more the type who calls it a good day if I remember to scrape off old mascara before piling on more.

Choking a bit on the words, I told her about the conversation with your daddy. "He just doesn't understand what I'm going through. I want to be pregnant so much. I feel this ache, this kind of intense longing down deep in my bones, you know? Every time I come near a baby, I swear, my uterus contracts. Like my body wants it as much as my heart does."

"Wait a second," Calista said. "Is it that you want to have a baby, or more that you just want to be pregnant?"

"It's kind of a means to an end, Calista," I said, slightly annoyed. "I can't exactly have a baby without being pregnant first."

"Well, duh," she said. "I only mention it because the whole time we were growing up, you swore you'd never have children. You thought people shouldn't bring more lives into the world because of war and pain and prejudice and all that jazz. And now suddenly you're all baby, baby, baby."

"It's not suddenly," I protested. "I started feeling this a while ago. Back when you had Davie." I practically moved in with Calista after his birth a year and a half ago, helping her, witnessing the peace that softened her when she looked at him or held him in her arms. I think it was then that it began to dawn on me that our children are our hope, our possibility of success, the ones who might bring a healing touch to the damage we've done to the world. They're what we have left to believe in. "All right, then," Calista said when I told her all this, "buck up and believe. Let it go. Stop pushing him. It'll happen when it's supposed to."

Your Auntie Calista has the ability to put these things into perspective. I've loved her since we were five years old, since that first day of kindergarten when she cut four inches off Tammy Beck's blond ponytail for saying I was ugly. She is the dearest kind of friend, the friend who helped me put in my first tampon, the friend who told me about blowjobs—that *blowing* doesn't really have anything to do with it. She's your auntie by soul relation only, but she's the closest thing to a sister I've ever known. So as far as I'm concerned, she's family. Family is supposed to know the worst things about you and love you anyway. Well, that's how it is with Calista and me. We piss each other off sometimes, but only because we know what buttons to push.

I heard Davie's muffled screaming in the background, then Mike's booming tenor insisting that Calista get off the phone and come put her son to bed. She sighed into the receiver, a small growl at the back of her throat. "*My* son, he says. God." She sighed again. "I gotta go, sweetie. Hang in there. I'll call you tomorrow."

As I sit here, shuffling papers, trying to organize all the work I have to get done tomorrow, I realize how right she is. I know I can't push your daddy into being ready, whatever that may mean. Something has to cross over in a person to make them believe they can do it, they can be somebody's mother or father, and it just hasn't happened to your daddy yet. But I know he wants it to happen, which at least means we're headed in the right direction. So, okay. I'll try to be patient. I will close my eyes, take a deep breath, and believe.

It's Monday morning and I am exhausted. Calista, Mike, and Davie came over for dinner last night and I went all out, making fresh bread and clam chowder from the secret recipe passed down to me by my Nana Cecille. Scrawled on an old pink note card in Nana's spidery script, the recipe calls for fresh clams—never canned—and an abundance of garlic. Nana swore the concoction traveled generations in our family before finally reaching her kitchen.

I wish Nana had lived long enough for you to meet her. She was my mother's mother, and for a few years of my early life I spent more time with her than I did at home. She'd dress me in one of Grandpa's old striped shirts with the sleeves rolled up, set me on a rickety wooden chair in front of her ancient gas range, and let me stir her thick chowder. I remember, even then, all those years after Grandpa had died, how those shirts filled my nose with the mellow spice of pipe tobacco. Soon after I turned five and my mother declared war on my father, I began sleeping over at

Nana's fairly often. On those occasions I liked to wear one of Grandpa's shirts as a nightgown, curling up next to Nana on her dusty old featherbed. Now I think that perhaps she liked it too. Maybe with me lying there, wrapped in the scent of him, in her dreams she could believe her husband was still alive, warming the space beside her.

The first time I asked what it was that made her chowder so special, Nana told me the secret ingredient was sea-fairy dust. From the pocket of her cherry-dotted apron she'd pull out a tiny bottle with an elaborate pewter screw-top, holding it up with reverence. "See this, peaches?" she'd say—she always called me peaches. "This is what your grandpa brought back from his fishing trips out on the sea. One awful night he got lost in a terrible storm. The waters were gray and angry, tossing him about, here and there. Out of nowhere, tiny fairies appeared and guided him home, then blessed him with this special dust. This is the magical-tasting stuff that makes up the wonder of this soup." She held me close to her billowy breasts and let me cradle the container in my palms. "Oh, Sarah, your nana loves you so much. Someday, when I go to live with the fairies, I will leave this to you. It will be yours to share with your own daughter. Your mother has never had much interest in cookin', has she? But you, my peaches, you are a gifted young chef." And then she'd let me sprinkle the fairy dust into the creamy, bubbling liquid. I promise, when you are old enough, to let you do the same.

Yesterday morning, while I chopped onions, garlic, and potatoes, I sent your daddy down to the Pike Place Market for clams. "You sure you don't want to go with me?" he joked as he pulled on his favorite purple sweatshirt. "Maybe we can convince the fish guy to let us toss orders again." I shook my head. "Hah. Fat chance, buddy. I'll see you when you get back."

Our junior year at the University of Washington, your daddy and I spent most Saturday afternoons strolling through the market, looking for bargains on fruits and vegetables to help supplement our starchy campus diet. One day he convinced the manager at one of the fish counters to let us learn how to toss orders. This is a huge tourist attraction in Seattle: The workers at some of the seafood vendors in the market are trained to launch customers' orders back and forth behind the counter, calling out remarks like "Long live the king!" as soon as a king salmon is airborne. If you ask me, it's a minor miracle how rarely they drop anything. Of course, your daddy was an immediate natural, effortlessly hurling rainbow trout through the air, calling out each order as if he'd been doing it for years. I, on the other hand, managed to drop practically every fish I touched. We ended up having to spend a fortune on filthy seafood we couldn't eat. But, god, how we laughed. Stomach-wrenching, can't-help-but-pee-in-your-pants laughter. That laughter has grown to be our backbone; it is what fuses us together.

Your daddy returned with beautiful, plump shucked clams for the chowder and an enormous bouquet of scarlet roses for me. He smiled shyly as he handed them over. "The old lady selling them said I looked like a man who loved a woman enough to give her these." He shrugged and raised his eyebrows.

"Couldn't argue with her." I thanked him with a kiss and a long, hard embrace. I have a thing about roses. The first time I was ever with your daddy, he scattered rose petals over the bed. He said the petals matched the shade of my lips, and when he lay on them, it would be as if I were kissing him everywhere at once. He's such a romantic. It's one of the things I love most about him: He's not afraid to be mushy, not even in front of other people.

Dinner was a hit, even Davie ate a few spoonfuls of chowder. Mostly, though, he threw bread around the kitchen and said, "Poo!"—his favorite new word. The men cleaned up while Calista and I sat in the living room. I told her I hadn't brought up getting pregnant to your daddy since the conversation last week. "Good girl," she applauded. "So, when do we start painting the nursery?" I laughed. "Didn't you say I wasn't supposed to push him?" Calista batted her eyelashes and reached to pull Davie away from the remote control and into her lap. "Painting isn't pushing him. Painting is merely upping the resale value on the house. At least, that's what you tell him."

Davie scrambled off his mother's legs over to me, wrapping his velvety, pudgy arms around my neck with an almost violent possessiveness. "Sawah mine!" he said. "Ba-ba Sawah?" Calista laughed and handed me his bottle, which he promptly snatched out of my hand and began to drink. "You sure love your Aunt Sarah, don't you, sweet boy?" She leaned back and sighed. "So. I'm thinking about signing Mike and me up for one of those 'put the spark back in your marriage' weekends."

Resting my chin on Davie's soft head, I gave her a concerned look. "Oh, yeah? Things that bad?"

She waved her hand over her lap as though she were shooing away a bug. "Oh, no. We're fine. Just marital maintenance garbage." She glanced toward the kitchen. "I don't hear the dishes cracking against each other anymore. Maybe we should check on them."

I smiled and shrugged. "Nah, they're big boys. Discussing the finer points of their basketball game yesterday morning, no doubt." Mike and your daddy have been friends since high school; I don't worry too much about whether or not they're entertaining each other. Though two more different men you probably won't meet—Mike is burly and your daddy is lean, aggressive while your daddy is peaceful—they tend to balance each other out. When they joined us a few minutes later, Calista grabbed Mike's hand and pulled him down next to her on the couch. "Did you see the roses Gavin bought for Sarah?" she asked him, nudging his ribs with her elbow.

Mike looked up at the flowers. Earlier, I had moved them from the coffee table to the mantel above the fireplace, safe from Davie's curious little fingers. "Yeah, I see them. They're nice. Very red."

Calista paused, then prodded, "But don't you think that was sweet of him? Surprising her with her favorite flowers for no reason?"

I glanced at your daddy, who was squirming a bit in his seat, uncomfortable for his friend. Mike chose to ignore Calista's insinuating tone, instead directing his attention to your daddy. "Mind if I grab myself another beer, there, Gav?" He extricated himself from Calista's grasp and moved back toward the kitchen.

Your daddy followed him, saying, "Think I could use another myself."

It drives me crazy when Calista stacks Mike up against your daddy. Back in college, when I first introduced her to Mike, I think she assumed his personality would be identical to your daddy's. She had listened to me rave about the new love in my life, and after meeting Gavin, she was astounded I had actually found a man who talked about his feelings, a man who wasn't terrified of his own tenderness. Then she learned your daddy had a best friend and immediately decided that that man *had* to be the one for her. Mike didn't stand a chance—when Calista sets her mind to something, not much deters her. So, despite their sometimes volatile relationship, Calista and Mike were married six months after your daddy and I were. Over the years the four of us have formed a comfortable alliance, but moments like the one last night remind me just how different our marriages are.

I turned my eyes to Calista, who was picking at the fringe of the pillow she held in her lap. Davie had finished his bottle and reclined farther against me, seemingly content to play with my fingers. "*That* was pleasant," I said, shifting his weight in my lap. "Planning anything for an encore?"

She frowned in response to my question. "What do you mean? I was simply pointing out how considerate Gavin is. Nothing more, nothing less."

"Okay," I conceded halfheartedly, knowing she believed that was all she had done. The men rejoined us a minute later, beers in hand, and nobody mentioned the flowers. We spent the rest of the evening discussing safe subjects: the building your daddy is designing for the Seattle City Council, and whether or not the Sonics will make it into the finals this season. I stroked Davie's duck-fluff hair until he fell asleep, eventually passing him into Mike's arms when they headed home.

We stood at the front window to watch them drive off, your daddy behind me, his arms wrapped tightly around my waist. He nuzzled my ear. "You look good holding that little boy." I smiled and turned around to face him, staying in his embrace. "I do?" He touched his forehead to my own and whispered softly, "Yeah . . . you do. A real natural. Think you might be able to teach me how to do it?"

This morning I am at home in my office, trying to get press releases written and mailed off for six different clients, but it is impossible to get my mind around anything other than the hope that your daddy might be about to change his mind.

I turned twenty-eight today and felt myself slide a little bit closer toward that dreaded thirty. When the time comes, I know it won't really be a big deal, but every woman I know worries about it so much, like being thirty is a disease that will silently overtake her, suddenly render her old and useless. I think maybe I've internalized this fear. Mostly, I try to ignore it, because honestly, I'm enjoying getting older. I feel like I'm finally settling into my own skin. Like I'm not so itchy with insecurity. The little lines that are forming around my eyes are simply traces of my memories, shadows of the laughter and tears I've shared with your daddy.

I said this to Calista this morning when she came over to our house, bearing birthday mochas and cinnamon rolls. She threw back her head to laugh at me. "I'm sorry, sweetie, but you're full of it. You hate aging just as much as everyone else. Wrapping it up in a shiny package of words and calling it pretty doesn't change the fact that we are getting *old*."

I didn't feel like arguing with her, but she's wrong. As time goes by, I really do feel more comfortable in my own body. More comfortable in my life. I think she disagreed with me because she is less comfortable in her own life than she'd like to believe. The other night when they were over for dinner is a perfect example. She'll mention problems with Mike, but as soon as I try to probe deeper, she immediately changes the subject. She does it all the time. There's some messy stuff brewing beneath the surface of their marriage, but she doesn't want to talk about it. She's a fixer: less talk, more action. Find a solution and ignore the pain. Personally, I think that when a woman pushes down dark, negative feelings, she becomes heavy with the weight of unspoken words. (I swear, the extra ten pounds I'm lugging around in my jeans is the manifestation of every bad feeling I've ever had and never been able to express to my mother.) Calista is carting around five years of little resentments toward Mike that probably could have been resolved if she were better equipped to talk about them and he were better equipped to listen. Instead, those piled-up grudges have built a wall between them. Their life together is not an abusive or horrible one, but it doesn't match Calista's perception of what a marriage should be.

Of course, I could say all this to her, and actually have hinted around the subject a few times, but honestly, I believe it's the kind of realization that's best for her to come to on her own if she is going to effect any real change in her life. You'll find that with your close girlfriends: When it comes to matters of their own personal search, anything you have to say will only tick them off if they haven't already realized whatever it is you point out. Mostly, it is safer to keep your mouth shut until they bring it up themselves.

So, to her comment, I simply smiled and said, "Well, whatever the case may be, I'm a year closer to thirty and still not pregnant. I don't think Gavin is ever going to be ready." Calista rolled her eyes but tried to be supportive. "You *know* he'll come around. It sounds like he's almost there from what you told me he said after we left Sunday night."

"I know," I said. But still, after she left to pick Davie up from the sitter, I spent the afternoon fantasizing about your daddy coming home and telling me my birthday present is that he's finally ready to be a father. When he walked through the door, I waited eagerly to hear those words.

"Happy birthday, sweetie," he said, hugging me close. "Can you get out of here for a little bit? I have to get a few things ready." Your daddy and I always want to outdo each other, both of us trying to come up with the best surprise for the other on his or her special day. I grabbed my coat and left for Kelly's, our favorite place in the neighborhood for ice cream. There I picked up two pints, one of Rocky Road for your daddy and another of Cinnamon Twist for me. I made a promise to myself to not be disappointed if his surprise didn't have anything to do with you. To pass the time, I wrote on a napkin, filling both sides with the words "I will not be disappointed."

After an hour or so, I came home to find little yellow Post-it notes pasted all over the house. There must have been a hundred of them. Your sweet father had taken the time to write down every special memory he kept of me, from the day I bashed into him in the college square until the night before, when we sat curled up together in front of the fire, sipping brandy and telling ghost stories. He wrote the things he loves best about me: the soft whistle of my nose when I sleep, the way I prop my legs up around both sides of the computer when I work at my desk, how I scratch his curly head when he's tired, and the way I rub small circles over his naked belly when he doesn't feel well. He wrote down how he felt when he saw me in my wedding dress, drifting down the stairs to meet him. "Sucker-punched" he wrote. "Completely disarmed —a victim forever of how much I need you." I'm going to frame that one and hang it over our bed.

I don't know where he was as I wandered the house, pulling off each note and reading his words with happy tears streaming down my face, but soon he was sliding his arms around me. We circled across the living room to no music, holding each other the way two people of very different heights do. For hours. We danced and held each other.

It has been the most amazing birthday of my entire life, even if we are still using birth control. Your daddy is asleep now, but I am sitting at my desk, going through the yellow slips of paper again, treasuring my life with this man. I had thought any surprise would pale next to his telling me he was ready for us to get pregnant. I was wrong. I will save those notes for you to read someday—someday when you are old enough to understand what a priceless gift really is.

I just got off the phone with your grandmother and I am starting to rethink this whole parenthood thing. My god. To think you might someday feel about me the way I feel about her fills me with dread.

She called to wish me a belated happy birthday, and after exhausting our usual repertoire about the weather and my "little publicity business," as she likes to call it—everything your grandmother doesn't like, she refers to as "little"—she asked, "When are you two planning on moving out of that little rental and into a real house?" I clenched my teeth. "It is a real house, Mother. And we bought it four years ago, remember? We like it here. We're staying." I waited for her response. "Well," she finally said, "I just thought Gavin might be concerned about how it looks for a successful architect to be living in that little bungalow, even though he obviously can afford something much more spacious." When I informed her that unlike *some* people, your daddy and I don't worry too much about what others think of the size of our house, she made an excuse about being late for dinner reservations and quickly ended the call.

Your grandmother has a thing about image. Almost immediately after she drove my father away, she married a man who could give her the luxurious lifestyle she was desperate to have. Enter my stepfather, David Devano, investment mogul. The two of them travel to faraway places almost eight months of the year, spending less and less time in the house he had built for her according to her direct specifications. If they don't grow completely tired of it and sell it off by the time you are born, you'll see this place. Gold-lined walls, cream carpet, priceless antiques from David's lifelong collection. It looks like a palace, a place to be cordoned off with velvet ropes and paraded throughout by tourists. It's not a home, it's a display.

She and David are in London now—she called me from the hotel he owns there—after spending the past three months hiking the mountains of Tibet. Of course, she didn't take the trip because she likes the outdoors, she did it so she can inform all her snooty society friends about her "months in Tibet" when she gets back. She'll let it roll off her tongue as if it were a trip to the market. "Oh, yes," she'll say, "when David and I spent our months in Tibet . . ." She's a braggart. She wants everyone to know what a lavish life she leads now that that dirt-poor first husband of hers is out of the picture. Like she has something to prove, even twenty years after the divorce.

Don't get me wrong. I love your grandmother. I just don't like her very much. There is a definite difference. I don't understand how money and prestige could be more important to her than being with the man she loves. She did love my father once, I'm sure of it, before the export company he worked for downsized and eliminated his cushy vice-president position. I remember them constantly kissing and laughing, my father coming up behind her and rubbing his whiskers into her neck, making her scream with pleasure. "Do it to me, Daddy," I'd squeal, "do it to me!" I saw how much he loved her and I wanted it for myself. What a loving man he was. It does not escape me how much your daddy is like my own. Affectionate, jovial, openminded. I think they would have been great friends.

When my daddy lost his job, we had to sell our beautiful house with the pool in the backyard and move into a one-bedroom apartment. I got to sleep on a fold-out couch in the living room. I was barely five years old; I thought it was an adventure. Macaroni and cheese was my favorite food, I didn't mind eating it every night. But your grandmother . . . she began to harden. Literally. Over the next year, every time I reached for her, she stiffened, her muscles solid and unyielding to my hesitant touch. I'm sure she did the same to my father; I never saw them kiss again. He'd reach out, and she'd wrench away from his grasp. "Carol, please," he'd say, his eyes pleading. She ignored him, sitting for hours at the kitchen table, looking through fancy architecture and travel magazines, showing me pictures and saying "See, Sarah? These are the things we could have had if your father hadn't gone and lost everything. Now we'll never have them. We'll never go to these places and see these wonderful things. These are what he promised me and this, this bug-infested hole, is what I got instead." She'd say this in front of him and he'd look as if she had just spit in his face.

"I swore the minute I got out of my parents' house, I'd never live like that again," she told me when my daddy wasn't around. "Like what?" I asked. She snorted and swept the apartment with an ugly sneer. "Like this, Sarah. With linoleum in the living room. Your nana and grandpa always tried to tell me how money didn't count more than love, but that was simply because they never had any money. When I was your age, I could never bring any friends over to play, I was so ashamed of our house—the way the wallpaper bubbled and peeled, how it always smelled like eggs." She wrinkled her nose as if she were there, smelling my nana's house again. I never thought Nana's house smelled bad; I liked eggs. Nana made them best sunny-side up, two on a plate, with a piece of bacon curved beneath like a brown, smiling mouth. Taking my small shoulders into her grip, my mother poured her eyes into mine. "I will not live like that again, Sarah, do you understand me? I absolutely refuse to do it."

The economy was bad and my father had been able to find only a production job in a machine shop. No chance of advancement. Your grandmother screeched at him constantly, demanding he find work in finance. "Work with money, have money!" she insisted. He would shrink at the sound of my mother's angry words. His shoulders that used to hold me up, high and proud, began to curl inward, as if he carried some unfathomable weight upon them.

This is when I began spending most of my time with Nana Cecille, and I suspect that my mother was out trying to reel herself in a new, rich husband during the long hours that my father worked. When I stayed with her, Nana never said a bad word about your grandmother, but sometimes I would catch her looking very sad. "What's wrong, Nana?" I'd ask. "Are your feelings hurt?" She would smile and pull me into her fluffy embrace. "No, no, my peaches. Your nana's only worried about her little girl." I scrunched my face up and said, "Little girl? You don't have a little girl! You're a grandma!" Nana laughed and corrected me. "Oh, yes, peaches, I do. Your mama is my little girl, and I will always worry for her, just as she will worry over you even when you are all grown-up. That's the way with mothers and daughters, no matter how many years go by."

During the rare times when I was at home with my parents, I remember watching as my father's skin turned steadily to ash. The day he left, it was two weeks before my sixth birthday. There was no food in the house. The power had been turned off because we could not afford to pay the electric bill. Again, I thought this was a romantic adventure, candles to light the rooms, soda crackers and peanut butter for dinner, but your grandmother did not. She sat with her arms crossed tightly over her chest, tapping her foot to a silent, staccato tune. When my daddy came home from work, she lit into him, told him to shape up, get a better job, give her what she wanted. I hid in the closet as she shrieked at him, clapping my hands over my ears to keep the horrifying sound of my father's tears from reaching my heart.

He left that night. Didn't even say good-bye. Walked out the door and disappeared. I didn't hear from him again until I was sixteen, living with my mother and David in a ten-bedroom house on Lake Washington. Life in that house came with all sorts of annoying rules: No shoes on the carpet, no food out of the kitchen, no animals. My mother had her money, but I couldn't have a dog.

My father called to wish me a sweet sixteen, and then told me he was dying of brain cancer. I didn't get to see him again, since my mother wouldn't pay for my plane ticket to Boston, where he was living, working as a security guard in a small museum. "Waste of time and money, Sarah," she said coldly. "Shake it off, the man hasn't amounted to a thing, just like I knew he wouldn't. Besides, what has he ever given to you?" I didn't cry—I hadn't seen him in ten years—but a small fire of resentment was ignited within me that day, fueled by your grandmother's icy nature.

I wish we got along better, but talking to her opens up the floodgates of the past. Our conversations make me feel like I'm drowning. She *is* my mother, and for a long time I tried to pretend she was not really that awful. It's your daddy who pointed out that blood does not necessarily form a lasting bond. "Look at us," he said. "We are closer than anything I could ever imagine and we don't have an ounce of the same blood. Relationships are built on emotional and intellectual connection, not genetics." I decided to try to accept your grandmother for who she is and let her live her own life, while I went ahead with mine.

It terrifies me that you will someday hate me. That you will look at me with that flaming anger in your eyes, that utter contempt for who I am. Is it unavoidable? I know that mothers can't always be perfect, and I know I'll certainly make mistakes. I just don't ever want to irreparably damage the connection between us. I swear, I will fight anything that threatens us. I will do whatever it takes to take care of you, to give you all the love you need to become a brilliant individual. Please know that when you finally enter into this world, I'll do everything I know to keep from becoming my mother.

Your daddy came home from work last night armed with two bottles: one of cheap champagne and another of fingernail polish. Dragon's Breath Red. When he walked through the door and saw me curled into my corner of the couch, he crooked his mouth sideways and said, "Hey, baby. I missed you today. Let's have some fun—take off your shoes." I told him I wouldn't do it if he expected me to drink champagne from my ratted-out sneakers. "Come on, trust me," he said. "Let me see your feet."

I hate my feet. Big mushroom toes bugging out from wide, flat acres of flesh. I probably would have been a goddess in the Cro-Magnon era. Your daddy knows I hate them, but even so, he's forever giving me foot rubs, caressing my arches with reverence, as though they were made up of some holy substance. But I wasn't in the mood for games. My biggest client had called that afternoon to tell me she was transferring to another PR company, some international outfit that would better launch her overseas career.

"Sorry," she had said. "I know you've stuck by me through some tough times, but this is really the best thing for my music. I'll be sure to recommend you to smaller artists." Yeah, right. Whatever, lady. Thanks a heap.

As I unlaced my shoes, I related this story to your daddy, who stuck out his lower lip and shook his head sympathetically. He shot the champagne cork into the kitchen. I heard it ping as it hit the refrigerator. "Poor baby," he said. "Let me kiss it and make it better." And there he went, after my feet. Rubbing and murmuring endearments to each of my little fungi phalanges, digging his thumbs into the thick pads of my heels while I drowned my sorrows, chugging champagne from the bottle.

So we sat, me on the couch and him on the floor, my legs hooked over his freckled shoulders so he could have better access to my feet. I loved your daddy's freckles the first time I saw them. There was something comforting in the light splattering of pale spots against his skin; it looked as though brown sugar had been sifted across his nose. His eyes are amazing too: the electric shade of fresh-cut grass. I don't tell him often enough how handsome he is; I think men probably need to hear those kinds of things just as much as women.

He rattled the nail polish bottle next to his ear like a maraca and began to paint each of my toes with exquisite care, using his index fingernail to wipe away any smudges along the cuticles. We passed the champagne back and forth until it disappeared. Your daddy kept tickling the underside of my foot, smiling as my legs twitched and jumped. "Careful," he said when he finished with the tiny shells of my pinky toes. "Stay very, very still so the polish can dry."

I lazed against the cushions with my eyes closed, feeling loose and tired as the alcohol oozed into my bloodstream, listening to the slow, deliberate echo of my heartbeat. Suddenly your daddy jumped up and ran down the hall to the bathroom, bringing my diaphragm and a pair of scissors back with him. "What're you doing with those?" I asked. He looked smug, smiled at me, and widened his eyes. "Makin' a baby, goofy, what does it look like?" Folding the rubber cup in half, he cut a big heart right out of the middle. "What do you say, Mrs. Strickland?"

It took me a moment to find my voice. "Hold it there, big guy. Three weeks ago you were certain you weren't ready, and suddenly you're mutilating my diaphragm? It doesn't make any sense." He shrugged and pulled out a tiny pair of pink socks, edged in lace, from his back pocket. "I know. I don't really get what came over me. I was walking along First Avenue on my lunch hour yesterday, saw these in a window, and felt this freaky urge to buy them. Then I figured if I was going to buy them, I'd better have a baby girl to wear them, right? That's where you come in. You keep saying how you have this feeling—you know, that woman's-intuition thing—that our first baby will be a girl, so I thought, Hey, who better to help me out?"

My mouth hung open. "Are you joking? Because I will kill you if you are. I swear, Gavin, I will kick your butt to Texas if you're kidding me." I asked him over and over if he was sure, until he took my face in his hands, looked me straight in the eye, and said,

"Sarah, I want this. Yeah, I'm scared, and I still don't know what being ready means, but, god . . . hon, I love you, okay? Feel the fear and do it anyway, or some such crap, right?" I kissed him, smiled, and said, "Right."

Today his careful paint job is gashed and bruised with carpet fibers, but I still haven't taken the polish off. I'm sitting here in my office, my insides wiggling with pleasure, wondering if either of our joinings last night will be the one to create you. I am certainly thinking of you, sliding my mind around you, trying to pull you in.

Yesterday I received a mysterious letter instructing me to meet a secret admirer in the downtown Hilton's bar that evening. Of course I recognized your daddy's chicken scratch, so I took the rest of the afternoon off to dress myself for the role of desired woman. Calista brought over a selection of sexy dresses, since your daddy has seen all mine. I chose a purple number that was somehow held together with spandex and dental floss; it took me twenty minutes to squeeze my butt into that thing. Your Auntie Calista and I wear pretty much the same size, but I tend to stick out in more places than she does.

As I stood in front of the bathroom mirror, fussing with my hair and makeup, Calista perched on the edge of the bathtub, watching me. She had plopped Davie inside the dry tub, handed him the toys she had brought along to keep him amused, then crossed her legs and propped an elbow on her knee. Cupping her chin in her hand, her eyes glittered wistfully. "I wish Mike did romantic crap like this," she said.

"I know," I said, trying to keep the exasperation I felt from leaking into my words. "But it's probably hard to be spontaneous with the rug rat to think about." I nodded my head toward Davie.

She smirked. "Yeah, but it's not like he couldn't plan a weekend for us and get my parents to watch Davie if he really wanted to. It simply would never occur to him to do it, you know?" Her expression brightened. "Hey, maybe you could get Gavin to say something to him, huh? Plant the idea in his unromantic little brain?"

"Oh, sure—*that'd* go over well," I said. "Just what every man wants: his best friend giving him pointers on how to seduce his wife."

"I know," Calista sighed. "I just don't know what to do. You'd think with how much the two of them hang out, some of Gavin's romantic nature would rub off on him."

I blotted my freshly painted lips on a square of toilet paper and turned to face her. "Men don't talk about their romantic natures, Calista. They talk about work and basketball and tools." I paused, thoughtful. "Tell me something. Do you know specifically what you want from Mike?"

She stood up, lifted Davie to her hip, and declared, "I want grand romance—candlelit dinners and love poems written on the bathroom mirror. I want him to remember that my favorite flowers are Gerber daisies and to bring me a wicker basket full of them on a Tuesday afternoon just because the sun is shining. I want breakfast in bed and diamonds for my birthday. I want it all."

"Well," I said gently, "maybe instead of hinting

around it, expecting him to figure all this out on his own, you need to *talk* to him."

She looked grim. "I shouldn't have to." She left a little while later, telling me to be sure to call her with the details of my evening out. This conversation with her frustrated the hell out of me; it's hard to watch her be unhappy and not be able to say anything that helps. Of course, it's always easier to see a solution when you're not standing in the middle of the problem.

Later, at the bar, your daddy approached me and pretended I was a stranger. "What's a nice girl like you doing in a dive like this?" was the pickup line he chose. I laughed and told him he should be grateful he knew I was a sure thing or else he'd be out of luck. I brushed his dark curls away from his forehead and kissed him softly. "Wanna dance, big fella?"

We spent an hour or so gliding across the dance floor, and then, at your daddy's urging, went to Kelly's for ice cream. The girl who waited on us wore a knit skirt that could have passed as a tube top; I caught your daddy stealing a glance at her annoyingly tight butt each time she passed our booth. Exasperated, I sighed heavily, hoping he'd take the hint to quit it without my having to say anything.

I hate it when he does things like that. I mean, I know it's normal to be attracted to other people—I get the whole "you can look at the menu but still eat at home" thing—but he shouldn't be doing it in front of me. It's a matter of principle.

The next time she sauntered past and his eyes followed her, I said lightly, "She's got a nice ass, doesn't she?" Your daddy's eyes snapped back to me, bright with guilt. "Uh, what?" he said, trying to pass it off like he hadn't been looking. "That waitress, she's got a nice ass," I repeated. "Maybe if you went over there and took a big handful, you'd be able to stop drooling over it." He sat back, arms outstretched, palms open to me. "Wow. Okay, you got me. I'm sorry." I licked a drip of ice cream from my spoon. "You should be. It's just rude, Gavin. I know it's normal to look, I look at other guys too, but I have the courtesy to not do it in front of your face, okay?" He nodded, reached a hand out to hold mine. "Forgive me?" I looked away, rolling my eyes. "I guess."

We sat in silence for a while, not looking at each other but still holding hands until your daddy finally spoke. "Ice cream will help you get pregnant, you know," he said with mock gravity. "But you have to eat it every day in order for it to work." Wanting to hold on to the romantic note upon which the evening had begun, I smiled with as much wickedness as I could muster. "Maybe I'm already pregnant." He stopped in mid-bite, looking up at me. "Are you? No way . . . it can't happen that fast. We just started trying, like, a week ago." He resumed eating his Rocky Road as I wiggled my eyebrows suggestively. "Hmmm . . . well, you never know. It only takes once, big boy."

I was only kidding your daddy, but honestly, there is a strange sensation in my body. I can't really explain it, but something feels different. Altered. Maybe you were conceived that night he painted my toes; maybe it did only take once. I don't know. I'm almost afraid to take a pregnancy test—I don't want to deal with the disappointment if it's negative. I called Calista this morning and told her how I was feeling. She told me to wait until my period was late. "Sweetie," she said, "you are the most impatient woman I have ever met. Calm down already. Come over here and watch Davie for me while I run some errands, would you? He's in a mood that'd convince any woman to get her tubes tied."

When I got over to their house, Davie screamed "Poo, Sawah!" and promptly threw his Brio train at my shins. Calista didn't even wait to hear about my night out with your daddy; she simply smiled and fluttered her fingers at us before practically running out the door. "Buh-bye! Have fun!"

The rest of the afternoon with Davie certainly pulled at my nerves, but I think the stress is different when it's not your own child. You don't get as frustrated because you know in a couple of hours you'll be giving that child back to his parents. And anyway, boys are harder than girls, I think. At least that's what Nana Cecille used to say. She had four older brothers, all of whom used to drive her crazy. "Whew! My peaches, those boys could make a mess! Mud and grass all over everything my mama and I washed: clothes, furniture, pots and pans. I swear. I loved my brothers, but I was honestly thankful when I had your mother that she was a girl. Didn't even try for another baby—I was happy with the one I got."

It seems strange to me how Nana was such a wonderful mother, bubbling with acceptance and love and generosity, and still your grandma turned out the way she did. I guess I can only hope the gene carrying parenting skills is the kind that stretches its legs, takes a running leap, and skips a generation.

You are inside me now. I know it with everything in my heart. My period is a week late. I feel the vitamins in my body being sucked to my belly, dancing around to nourish your every need. I can't feel you, and I know you're no bigger than the head of a pin, but, sweet baby, you are with us.

This morning, after I peed on a stick and felt my heart curve into a smile as I watched the plus sign turn pink, I went to your nursery. The sunlight sprayed over the walls in a watery mist, and I remembered walking into this same room four years ago, the day the real estate agent showed us the house. We had looked at ten or so homes over the course of a month, and were spending every waking moment trying to figure out how we were ever going to afford closing costs and agent fees on top of the down payment we had barely managed to scrape together. Your daddy's new job with the firm Parker & Parker had come with a substantial raise, but I had only recently gone from doing freelance press releases for local musicians to running my own PR business out of our apartment. I had only two clients and was lucky if the checks came in on time. Money was tight.

The house was nestled in the small Queen Anne neighborhood, and as we pulled up in front of the only house on the block with a for-sale sign, I noted the towering knotted oaks that lined the street. They twisted high and strong, each seeming to tell its own story; I immediately felt the urge to sit down and listen to the wisdom of their years.

When we approached the small brick structure, our agent emphasized closet space and the cozy country kitchen, but what spoke to me as soon as I entered was this room. I walked right to it, past the living room and down the hall to the wide-open windows; I fell in love with the window seat that looked out over the deck to the backyard. I had dreamed of such a room for myself when I was a child, a room that lent a view of the world yet safety from it. "This is it," I told your father, "we have to buy this house." He smiled at me, that crooked, half-lipped grin of his that said he thought I was a kook but would gladly sacrifice a limb if it meant he could give me everything in the world, then turned to the agent to make an offer. Your daddy says we were lucky that the previous owners wanted to unload the place quickly and were willing to settle for a little less than they had been looking for. I like to believe the house was meant for us and any offer we had made would have been accepted. That's what Nana would have said. "When things are meant to happen, they just do," she told me once. "Remember, peaches, there's not a thing we can do about most happenings in this world except be thankful when good times come to us." I remember she paused a moment, then continued with a wistful smile on her face. "Of course, we should be thankful for the bad times too, I suppose. That's when we tend to learn the most."

I had barely glanced at the rest of the house before seeing your room, but as I then wandered through, shining cherry-wood floors, built-in bookshelves, and a river-stone fireplace only served to confirm my decision. Yes, it was small, three cracker-box bedrooms, one bathroom, no dining area, and, as we would soon discover, wiring that permitted the use of only one appliance at a time. It needed a good scrub, new paint, and a few nuts and bolts, but overall it has turned out to be the perfect home for us, and, soon, for you.

The day we moved in, I started the unpacking while your daddy made a trip to the hardware store. He returned without the garbage cans I had asked for —if your daddy doesn't write something down, he will most likely forget it—and instead dragged a spindly, sorry-looking Japanese cherry tree and two garden spades into the backyard. The tree was a fall clearance special, but the garden guy told your daddy that if we got it in the ground that day, it should make it through the winter. It was getting dark, and after a long day of hauling boxes and furniture, the absolute last thing I felt like doing was planting a tree. Your daddy slunk up behind me, kissing my neck and nuzzling my ear with words of endearment about rites of passage and needing to mark our life together. Before I knew it, we were digging by twilight. Your daddy did most of the work. I mostly supervised, and when the last bit of dirt was patted down, your daddy took my hand and asked the starlit sky to bless our new home as well as the life we would live within it. That tree grew strong over the next couple of years, and now, little one, it is the centerpiece of our yard, the first thing you'll see each morning when you rise from your bed.

So I stood in your room, remembering this, dreaming of your smell, your smile, your bubbling laughter that will fill our lives. I can't wait to feel you move inside me. To know there's a life growing in my body, to touch you, to sing you silly songs. You won't mind my horrible voice, will you? You will love me without question simply because I am your mommy.

I haven't called your father yet to tell him; I want to hold this precious knowledge to myself for a while, cupping it close to me. I know that you are barely a bundle of cells, a grain of rice, but within you floats such magic, the ability to grow and develop into our child. Our little girl. I can't stop imagining you as sugar and spice. Your daddy calls it woman's intuition, but I'm not sure that's it. I just know. Maybe you are sending me a message, some kind of mental telepathy. Nana Cecille used to say that there are things sensed between mothers and their children without a word ever being exchanged between them. I tend to believe she was right.

Your daddy almost spontaneously combusted when I told him I'm pregnant. I waited until he got home from work, and when I hugged him and whispered in his ear that he was going to be a daddy, he danced a little jig in the living room, then came over to lay his ear on my stomach, where you are living. He kissed you. Did you hear him tell you that he couldn't wait to meet daddy's little girl? "Wait," he said. "Wait right here, don't go anywhere. Don't call anybody. I'll be right back."

He returned from the corner market with two perfectly budding crimson roses, one for me and one for you. "You know," he said as I put the flowers in a crystal vase, "I thought I'd be more freaked out. I mean, I thought I'd need a stiff drink or something, but really, I'm just so happy." His grin was almost wide enough to see his molars. "A daddy. Wow. Holy crap. You've got a baby inside you, Sarah. *A whole other person.* And we made her, you and me, boom, just like that. It's amazing."

Yes, it is amazing. It's also amazing how you are making me throw up everything I eat. I'm trying to give you nourishment and all you do is reject it. I can barely manage crackers, and then suddenly I'm dying for a steak. Your daddy laughs, holding my hair back as I toss up my breakfast into the toilet, telling me I should just go back to my regular diet of chocolate milk and Pop-Tarts and then you'll probably stop making me puke. But then he makes me tea and dry toast, wipes my face with a cool damp cloth, and tucks the blanket back up under my chin before he leaves for work. Yesterday he brought me breakfast in bed: two strawberry-frosted Pop-Tarts and a bowl of my favorite fruit, sliced ripe mango. It's two months past the fruit's season, but when I asked him where he found it, all he'd say was "I got people everywhere, baby. . . ." Your daddy would like to think he's a comedian.

He's calling me fifty times a day from the office to see how I am doing. "Hanging in there," I tell him, "barfed up a lung a couple minutes ago, but otherwise I'm just dandy." He says being cranky isn't going to make me feel better. I told him it was already making me feel better. What does he know? But, baby, I mean it, I've got to get some sort of vitamins in you. Back off with the nausea, okay?

We waited until Halloween to tell Mike and Calista that you are finally on your way. Davie was spending the weekend with his grandparents in Everett, trick-or-treating in their safely gated retirement community, so I asked your daddy if we could skip his company's party this year. I told him there was no way to top last year's costume anyway. He glued Barbie dolls all over his clothes and went as a chick magnet. "Of course I can top it," he said. "I was thinking of wearing one of your slips with a picture of Freud stitched on the front." I do wonder sometimes if I should be concerned about the spot in his brain that comes up with these things.

But after a little cajoling from me he agreed it would be more fun to hang out with Mike and Calista, handing out candy to all the little kids in our neighborhood. The four of us ordered in Thai food, and after refusing Mike's offer to get me a beer, I made the big announcement. "I'm on the wagon, kids," I said. "The bun is officially in my oven." Calista managed to lose a mouthful of pad thai down the front of her shirt. "Oh, my god!" she squealed. She playfully socked your daddy's shoulder. "Way to go, stud!" Mike reached over to shake your daddy's hand, then got up and hugged me tight, lifting me out of my chair in his enthusiasm. Calista fell into her spiel of first-trimester advice, reminiscing about her experience with Davie. "You have to start prenatal vitamins right away," she informed me. "Have you bought any yet? What about calcium? I know you don't get enough of it. You should get some supplements, plus some folic acid and iron tablets. Buy one of those daily vitamin holders— you know, the ones with little cartridges for all seven days of the week?—and fill it up. I'll take you to the health food store, because they have cheaper prices than the pharmacies. Do you have a doctor yet?" I listened to all this as patiently as possible. I guess she forgot I was there when she was pregnant with Davie; I witnessed the whole process including his birth—I took notes.

Even after telling Mike and Calista the news, it's still hard for me to believe that you're inside me. I keep checking my belly to see if I am showing, but so far nothing but the usual pudginess. Although my uterus does feel hard, and besides all the puking, you're making me have to pee every ten minutes, which I've heard is pretty standard. But most of all, I am exhausted enough to sleep standing up. I was in line at the grocery store the other day and the woman behind me had to nudge me when it was my turn at the checkout. I don't think I have ever felt so tired in my life. My blood feels weighted down by hot lead; it practically takes a bulldozer to scoop my butt out of bed. Calista says that if I think I am tired now, just wait until after you are born.

I really don't mind so much. I nap when I need to and let the voice mail get my messages. My clients get slightly annoyed when I don't get back to them right away, but one way or another, I'm getting the job done. Press kits are sent, phone calls are made, interviews are set up. Honestly? I'm relieved your daddy and I agreed that I'd close the firm after you are born. Believe me: Owning your own business tends to take over a larger corner of your life than you had originally planned. Of course, if I feel the need, I can always take on a few low-maintenance clients when you are old enough for school, but for now, I'm looking forward to the sabbatical.

Your father says I should just quit now, since I confirmed with Dr. Foster that you are on the way. Much to Calista's delight, I have decided to see the same doctor she went to when she was pregnant with Davie. I liked the idea of seeing this particular woman, since she started out as a midwife. She told me she chose to enter medical school so she could become one of those rare doctors who is willing to work in concert with midwives. She was also tired of the doctors making all the money for the same job she was doing. She's a solid woman, thick and close to the ground. Her coarse gray hair is blunt cut below her ears, not quite brushing the bulk of her rounded shoulders. I told Calista that Dr. Foster's build makes me feel safe, as if with her strength she would be able to handle anything that might go wrong during your delivery. I look at her and think one word: capable.

At my first appointment she put me through

about a zillion blood tests to make sure everything was going well. All my hormones are doubling like they are supposed to, and my blood sugar is fine, but I'm still terrified that I might do something wrong and you'll be hurt. I'm afraid the energy that glows from the computer I sit in front of most of the day is somehow damaging you. I want to wear a mask to protect you from the pollutants that overwhelm the air we breathe. Maybe I should stop using the microwave; I read somewhere that they might be harmful to a fetus. I am desperate for you to be healthy; please, let me eat some vegetables!

O kay, baby, I have to be honest—I'm getting a little scared, a little overwhelmed, wondering if this motherhood thing was such a good idea. What if I drop you on your head and give you brain damage? What if you don't want to breast-feed and we don't experience the bonding we are supposed to? What if, no matter how hard I fight against it, I end up exactly like my mother? I called Dr. Foster earlier today, and she reassured me that all mothers have these concerns and healthy babies continue to be born all the time. She also told me that it's really the skin-to-skin contact of breast-feeding that stimulates the bonding process; so now I'm going to insist that your father get naked with us at least once a day so he can have that intimate bonding too. Dr. Foster said that was a fabulous idea and even if your daddy thinks I'm nuts to ask it of him, he should go along with it to make me happy. If anything, to keep me from kicking his butt around the room.

Your daddy, by the way, is going absolutely crazy

buying you things. There is already a baseball glove and a miniature mechanics set waiting for your arrival, because your father believes in instructing girls in all necessary functions of the world, like being able to fix a flat tire and change the oil in your own car. When he first met me, he was appalled by my lack of technical know-how, so as a result we've spent way too many exasperating hours in the garage bent over greasy engines. I suppose if someone held a gun to my head, I could probably tighten a few bolts, and I'm pretty sure I've mastered the correct way to twist a socket wrench, but honestly, mechanics don't make much sense to me. Your daddy gets a bit condescending when I'm slow on the uptake, sighing and rolling his eyes, flabbergasted by my ignorance. He's planning on teaching you all the workings of an inner combustion engine as soon as you can pick up a wrench, so be prepared.

So far he is being very understanding of the effects you are having on me. I'm still fairly cranky, and I have developed what Calista calls "pregnancy nose"— my sense of smell has suddenly turned up to its highest capacity. Last night your daddy was lying next to me in bed, snoring lightly, when I shook him until he woke. "Wh-wh-what is it, baby? You okay? Everything all right? Are you sick?" He reached over to pat my belly absentmindedly as he turned over to doze back off. I shook him again. "Gav? There's something reeking in the kitchen, would you please go get it out of the house?" He didn't answer me, so I poked him in the back, down by his kidneys, until he sat straight up. "Ow! Would you quit? What's wrong?" I sighed. "There's something stinking in the kitchen, probably

in the garbage. I can't sleep, it's keeping me awake."
He slowly closed and opened his eyes a few times, like
a large, sleepy owl, and tried to understand what I was
saying. "You want me to empty the garbage? It's three
A.M., Sarah. I'll do it in the morning." Grabbing his
arm, I pleaded, "Please, hon? It's driving me crazy."
He grumbled good-naturedly for a minute. "Loopy
pregnant lady . . . smelling things . . . waking me
all up . . . making me go outside . . ." Then shuf-
fled to the kitchen in his underwear. I heard the back
door open, then close. I was asleep before he even got
back into bed.

This was especially considerate of your daddy,
since he hates to be woken up by anything other than
his own volition. During the first months of your life I
want him to bring you to me from your crib when
you need your nighttime feedings. Calista did that
with Mike, and he told me it made him feel much
closer to Davie, like he was part of the whole nurtur-
ing process. I'm concerned your daddy won't be too
excited about two-hour-interval feedings, but he is already so crazy about the idea of you, I'm sure once
you are here, he'll leap out of bed just for the opportunity to cradle you in his arms. Although I think he
might be a little frightened of how fragile you will be;
he keeps asking me about the spot on your head where
your skull won't be entirely fused together. "Sarah-
bara . . . where's the soft spot, again?" he asks,
thumbing through the pregnancy books I borrowed
from Calista. "In the front of the head or the back?
Should I even touch it?" He's trying to learn everything he can so he can be as much a part of bringing
you into the world as it's possible for a man to be.

Which I love. But he's convinced that just because I'm a woman, I've got all this information encoded in my brain or something, when the truth is, I have just as many questions as he does. What if we don't know what to do to comfort you? What do we do if you have colic? Or a diaper rash? There is so much we have to learn to be the kind of parents we want to be. But don't you worry your sweet little head. Someone will always be there to hold you when you cry out in the night.

Thank you so much for easing up on the food rejection. I have cut down the throwing-up to once or twice a week. You seemed to do especially well at Thanksgiving, when I ate piles of mashed potatoes with turkey gravy. My butt's spreading like soft butter as we speak, thank you very much. I've gained only eight pounds so far, but I'd better watch it, or we'll have some seriously long walks in store for us when you get here. I've tried to get out to do a couple of miles every day, but I'm still so tired, all I feel like doing is lying on the couch. So that is exactly what I've been doing.

We went over to Calista and Mike's for the holiday, and once again, as with every special occasion we spend at their house, Calista insisted on doing the whole meal by herself. When we have them over, I always appreciate it if she brings a salad or dessert, even if I don't ask her to. I've never once said "Don't bring anything." But when I called to discuss it with her, she proclaimed, "I've got it under control, Sarah. I've got the whole menu planned and shopped for, beginning to end, so don't worry about it."

"I can't even bring my famous brownie cheese-cake?" I asked.

"You don't have *cheesecake* at Thanksgiving, Sarah. You have pumpkin pie and maybe an apple tart." For her, that logic signaled the end of the discussion.

Now, granted, your auntie could give Martha Stewart a run for her money. No traditional turkey stuffing for this woman: Hers is always chock full of apples and sausage and rosemary, her mashed potatoes creamed with roasted garlic and thyme. She's a decorating freak too. Her home is kissed with bouquets of candles and flowers and seashells; each room is tinted in perfect Easter-egg hues, and breezy linen drapes soften the windows. She's the one I consult when I get the urge to rearrange our furniture. But still. I told your daddy how ridiculous she was being about the whole thing, and he sympathized. "Sounds like she knows how she wants things to be, and if they don't turn out that way . . ." He raised his eyebrows, tilted his head, and let his voice trail off. "Well, let's just say Mike has commented on it a few times."

So, since I wasn't allowed in the kitchen with Calista and Mike, I spent most of the day watching your daddy play with Davie, treasuring the gentleness of his touch, his patience with the little boy's fits of frustration. Although I do believe your daddy was having more fun with Davie's toys than Davie was. As Davie busied himself repeatedly crashing a yellow dump truck into the coffee table, your daddy bent two pliable alligator figures into various formations. "Look," he said, holding the toys up to me. "Hostage alligator." He had wrapped one alligator's arm around the chest of another, with the first alligator holding one of his forefeet up to the second's head like a gun. "Oh, boy," I said, rolling my eyes and laughing. "Somebody should give you your own TV show."

Later, at one point during their play, your daddy caught me watching him and Davie, and came over to lay one hand on my belly and the other to my cheek. How well he knows me. He knew I was thinking about what a wonderful daddy he will be to you. His touch was a promise. Calista emerged from the kitchen and witnessed this moment between us; I could almost see her insides twinge green. I thought about what your daddy had said earlier, about her having ideas of how things should be, and I felt momentarily guilty for having with your daddy what she so desperately wants with Mike. But then I thought, Wait a minute, she doesn't have it that bad; it's just that in her mind, if Mike doesn't show his love the way she thinks he should, then he's doing it wrong. It's like she's blinded by the standards she has created. She can't see the preciousness in the way Mike helps her in the kitchen, chopping onions and grating cheese; the way he changes Davie's diapers or feeds his son a bottle without a word of prompting from her; the way he always picks up milk on the way home from work because he knows they'll need it by the next morning. Those gestures may not be the grand romance she's looking for, but maybe it's the only way Mike knows to show her he loves her. It struck me how much happier Calista might be if for one moment, instead of focusing on all that Mike fails to be, she could open her heart and see all that he is.

At my eight-week checkup with Dr. Foster, she said that you are starting to look like an actual baby —about one and a quarter inches long. I could easily cup your entire body in the palm of my hand. How fragile you must be, yet how utterly perfect. Your heart is beating now. Do you wonder what it is, this thumping inside you?

I have not felt you yet, even though Dr. Foster said you are able to move, that you are training your muscles and practicing your motions, getting them ready for life outside my womb. Even so, I woke up terrified the other night, positive that you were not really inside me, that you were never there, that I imagined you. But your daddy reassured me; hadn't we just heard your tiny heartbeat in Dr. Foster's office? He cuddled me closely and sang to us, which, despite his voice, I appreciated. Have you heard your father sing to you in the mornings? He's even worse off in the vocal harmony department than I am, don't you think? His musical taste is sketchy too. Somehow, I don't believe you'll be a fan of the drum-heavy, electric guitar–laden tunes he loves. I am playing Thelonius Monk for you, and Sarah McLachlan. I wonder which you like better?

I hope you are warm and cozy; I am doing everything I know to keep your world healthy and bright.

I cried today because I dropped an entire carton of yogurt on the floor. I crumbled to the linoleum and sobbed for an hour over the loss. Your daddy came home to find me there, tearful and clutching the slippery mess. Can you believe he laughed at me? He has no idea how completely overcome I am right now. I swing back and forth between elation and sorrow, with no control over how I express what I'm feeling. He does not understand how it is to be carrying a life inside you. To feel as if you're possessed; overtaken by some new, multiple-personality self. I tried to explain this to him, but no words seemed to make any sense, and I just kept crying until your daddy reached out to me and pulled me to his lap on the floor.

He rocked me gently and ran his hand over my hair and told me over and over what a wonderful mother I will be. He held me until my tears slowed to hiccups and then lifted me to a kitchen chair. We talked as he made us scrambled eggs and pancakes for dinner. He told me about the new receptionist at his office who tried to put Wite-Out on the computer screen and the big remodel account with the Seattle Aquarium he had managed to land for the firm. Mr. Parker, Sr., had come into your daddy's office to personally congratulate him. "Looks like it will be a good Christmas bonus year," your daddy said, smiling.

These are my favorite times with your daddy, the simple coming-home-from-work-and-telling-each-other-about-our-day times. Sharing the little things about our days—how the cashier at the grocery store had a pimple the size of Texas on his nose, or how the bum in Pioneer Square bent over and showed enough crack to rival the Grand Canyon—is what pulls us together. It fills in the empty spaces between us.

After dinner, as we sat in the living room watching mindless sitcoms and reading the evening paper, I was overcome by a craving for ice cream. I casually suggested to your daddy that we head over to Kelly's and split a hot fudge sundae. He looked at me, surprised. "That's just weird. I was sitting here, thinking how incredibly good a big pile of ice cream would taste." I went over to pull him up from his spot on the sofa. "Do you want potato chips too? Because I want some potato chips. The salt and vinegar kind, okay? Let's stop at the store on the way home."

In the car, with his right hand stuck deep inside a bag of chips while his left held both a double scoop of Rocky Road and the steering wheel, your daddy chuckled. "We'd better be careful, or we're both going to be huge by the time this baby is born." I frowned. "Well, it's okay if I get fat. I'm supposed to get fat." He looked at me like "yeah, right," and I said, "No, really. Dr. Foster gave me a nutrition guide. A little sugar and salt now and then won't do anything bad. Everything in moderation, right, baby?" I said, patting you softly. "Everything in moderation."

It suddenly hit me this morning, how unfathomable it is that I'm going to be a mother. Calista says not to worry, that I will know how to mother instinctually, but will sometimes flub everything up despite my best intentions. Some best friend, huh? She is actually there for me in many ways that your father can't be, since she understands what I'm going through. We went shopping for maternity bras on Tuesday night, my already substantial breasts are swelling past the point of reason; sore and tingling every day now, and she teased me endlessly about my new, darkly shaded nipples. They have always been pink, practically invisible.

"They look like ginger snaps," she giggled as she stood next to me in the dressing room, clutching a handful of heavy-duty elastic and cotton bras.

I groaned and covered my breasts with my hands. "Don't tell Gavin that, or he'll use it as another excuse to put his mouth on them. I hate to say it, but I absolutely cringe every time he even *looks* like he might want to touch them."

"Get him a blow-up doll for the next couple of months," she teased. "Because, believe me, sweetie, you won't feel like doing it until at least the middle of your second trimester." She held up one of the bras she was holding. "Here. This is the one you should get." When I tried it on and told her it was itchy, she said, "Itchy boobs are going to be the least uncomfortable part of your body over the next couple of months. They already ache, so a little itch isn't going to hurt you any. Don't be a wuss."

"You're kinda pushy," I told her playfully.

"Yeah, well," she said, "it's all a part of the glorious bitch that is me. Get over it and go pay for this bra so we can get some food."

Times like this with Calista, pushiness and all, remind me just how much I cherish our friendship. I adore your daddy, but there is something between women that men can never match. Even though it's hard for the two of us to find time for the careful attention our friendship deserves, I believe that when we put the energy in, something amazing comes back to us. Sometimes I long for the time when a woman's job consisted of gathering daily with the women in her life: sewing, cooking, gardening, watching each other's children, spending their days talking and laughing and healing each other's wounds. The quilting way of life, Nana called it. "It's not the act of making a quilt that really matters," she'd say. "It's the time women used to have together. They were each other's strength."

I think that when women allow themselves to

bond, something mystical and powerful occurs; a connection with the spiritual and natural world ignites with our holding each other up instead of trying to tear each other apart. Maybe someday we can return to this link between women. Maybe you will be the woman who will bring us all together. Who knows? You can be anything your precious heart desires. Anything at all.

Winter . . .

I let voice mail pick up early today so I could brave the malls and look for a present for your daddy. He's impossible to shop for; when he wants something, he usually just goes out and buys it. A few years ago I tried to get him to agree to a buying freeze three weeks before any significant holiday so I could actually get him a gift he wanted, but his self-control is not the greatest. Yesterday he came home with the bench grinder I was planning on getting him this year, so two days before Christmas, I was back to square one.

Northgate Mall was packed, hundreds of people milling from store to store, weighted down by children and packages and frustration. In front of Nordstrom's I saw a little girl sitting on Santa's lap and I thought of you. I imagined dressing you up in a lace-edged red velvet dress with a matching hat and taking you to tell your most heartfelt wishes to the bearded old man. Will you be frightened? Will you cry like some of the children standing in line, terrified of being made to sit in a stranger's lap, or will you walk right up and tug on his beard to check for authenticity like your daddy did when he was a little boy? I stood there for quite a while, watching and listening as the children made the journey through the line, but then had to fight the tears when a little boy told Santa that all he wanted for Christmas was to have his daddy back living in the same house with him and his mommy. Sadness rested its mask across his mother's face, and I had to walk away.

I wandered the stores, picking up various tools, sweaters, books on architecture, and other items I've chosen for your daddy's gifts a hundred times before and finally decided to leave the godforsaken mall and head downtown. After finding a miraculous parking spot beneath the Monorail, I walked along Fourth Avenue and happened upon a tiny closet of space, a small shop with no name. The inside was dark except for three table lamps placed across the two glass display cases, their yellow, cloudy shine illuminating just enough for me to see wood and stone filling the shelves. The air was steeped in tobacco. An old man held up his hand in greeting and wobbled over to stand behind the case in front of me. He had to be close to ninety years old; the lines around his eyes and mouth were etched deep, though the rest of his face was smooth, thin as parchment paper. His eyes were bright, the fragile shade of forget-me-nots.

I made some joking comment about having an impossible man to shop for, and he simply reached inside the case and pulled out a goblet carved of a shining dark wood with two small rings intertwined together and around the stem. The man told me the whole piece was carved from one branch of a cherry tree and symbolized the joining of two souls destined to be together forever. Then he set a dusty bottle of fifty-year-old Scotch next to the goblet and said any man would be thrilled to have a wife who would buy him such fine liquor. I told him I didn't know if your daddy even liked to drink Scotch, to which the old man replied, "Whether he likes it or not does not matter, my dear. Any man knows the quality of such a gift, and to have a woman who knows this as well, ah"—the old man lifted up his hands and shrugged his shoulders—"this is a man who will know how much you love him. It is in your eyes, you know, I wouldn't let just any woman buy this drink. It is in your eyes how deep your love for this man goes."

I stopped by Calista's on the way home to tell her what the old man had said and show her what I'd bought. "Well," she mused doubtfully, turning the goblet in her hand and moving her glance to the bottle of Scotch in my grasp. "They're not things I'd have picked out. Don't you usually get him tools or something?"

"Yeah," I said, "but something told me the old man might be right, you know? And with the baby on the way, Gavin might need to be reassured of how much I love him."

Calista sniffed. "Whatever you say, sweetie. Did you remember to ask about the guy's return policy?"

Smiling, I answered her. "I don't think I'll need it."

Three years ago your daddy and I started a tradition of camping out in front of the Christmas tree. Curling up next to a roaring fire on Christmas Eve, we doze off and on till morning, toasty beneath the heavy warmth of our sleeping bags. Before opening presents, your daddy whips us up some breakfast. Sometimes we'll spend the latter part of the day with Calista and Mike and their extended family, but mostly we like to be at home. It's certainly less stressful than the horror stories we hear about other people's day, spent enduring relatives with whom they'd rather not share blood, let alone a meal.

This year Christmas blew in on a gray-soaked morning. I woke to the sound of rain exploding like tiny liquid bullets against the living room windows, accompanied by the rich scents of cinnamon French toast and hickory-smoked bacon. I've been getting an automatic reaction to what I eat lately: Baby says yes or baby says no. You definitely went for this meal, but

I do have to say how strange it is having someone else control your taste buds.

Calista and Mike called first thing to wish us a joyful day. Davie got on the line and sang us his wordless, garbled rendition of "Jingle Bells." His high-pitched giggles of pleasure made me realize that next year your daddy and I will have you here with us, cuddled in front of the tree. We will probably be like Calista and Mike, spending every nickel we have spoiling you with toys you'll ignore while you play with the boxes in which they came. "We're headed to the grandparents' houses for the next couple of days," Mike said. "We'll call you when we get back, okay?"

After we ate breakfast, we sat on the floor to open presents. Your daddy absolutely loved the goblet and the Scotch. Especially the Scotch. He kept saying "Jesus, I can't believe you got me a fifty-year-old bottle of Scotch. Jesus. That is just the coolest thing, baby. It's just the coolest thing!" He wouldn't stop kissing me. When he finally calmed down enough to give me the small box he had been hiding at his office, he suddenly turned shy and said he hoped it was an okay gift. He picked it out without any help from Calista. I carefully pulled the tape from the gold foil paper, knowing it drives your daddy nuts how long I take to open a present. I don't know why I prolong the process, it's only that sometimes the anticipation of a gift is more thrilling than the gift itself.

To be honest, I was surprised there was only one box from your daddy; he usually gets me twenty different little things instead of one big thing. I've tried before to explain that more is not always better, that one well-thought-out gift can be more meaningful than several impulse buys, but the multi-gift-holidays had continued. When I lifted the velvet top off the box in my hand, I knew he had finally heard me. Nestled against the green tissue was a necklace, a rounded gold pendant with three molded figures, two parents cradling an infant. A brilliant half-carat diamond rested at the base of the charm, catching the twinkling lights from our Christmas tree and shooting off a kaleidoscope of rainbow hues across the floor. I could not stop the tears, and I reached to touch your daddy's cheek, to hold his eyes with my own and somehow convey the intensity of my feelings. "I know, Sarah," he said. "It's all right, it's okay, baby. I know."

I was feeling so peaceful, so open-hearted and full of love, I decided to call your grandmother in London to break the big news. "Surprise!" I said. "Merry Christmas—I'm pregnant." There was silence. "Oh," she finally said, her voice flat. "Well. Did you plan on having that happen? I certainly hope Gavin isn't expecting you to stay in that little house now. You'll need a room for the nursery, and a nanny, right?"

I should have known by then to stick to e-mailing her—no tones of voice to contend with. She threatened to come and stay with us before she and David head off next week for a six-month stay in Australia, but I quickly talked her out of that, explaining that we were definitely planning to stay in our "little" house, the house that inexcusably lacks a guest room with its own private bath. She sighed. "I suppose you're right, dear. Well, don't gain too much weight. Having a baby can destroy your body if you're not careful. Trust me, I know." The woman drives me insane.

Your daddy and I spent the rest of the weekend working on your nursery. He went shopping with me today so we could find the after-holiday bargains—you should have seen him in the children's department, gingerly picking up stuffed animals and toys, then asking me, "Is this one okay? Do you think she would like this?" It was adorable.

When we got home, he finished applying a second coat of robin's-egg blue to the walls in your room, sealing the door off with heavy towels and duct tape so that I wouldn't breathe in any fumes. It should be safe for me to enter in a couple of days, and we can start arranging everything for your arrival. I know we still have six months, but I feel like I can't get ready for you soon enough. I've already been trying on third-trimester maternity clothes, strapping on the fake belly one store provided to see what I'll look like, spending hours in the dressing room with tentlike dresses and really big panties. The saleslady smiled at me and shook her head. "This must be your first," she said. I can't help it. I can't stop this excitement, this obsession with what I should be eating and doing and thinking and wearing. I just want to be ready, to do everything possible to make your entrance into this world a grand occasion.

I love that every time your daddy passes by, he reaches a hand out to cup around my belly. Do you feel him touch you? Do you hear him when he places his lips against the small, firm softball of my stomach and tells you his goofy little stories about his trip to the gas station or his Saturday morning basketball game? I've read that you can already hear everything we are saying, and that even now you react to your environment. Dr. Foster said the sound of my voice travels through my bones, so I guess it's more that you feel the words than actually hear them. I tell your daddy to get very near you so you can feel the vibration of his words as well. So when you come out of me and hear his voice, you'll say, "Oh, yes, I know that man, that's my daddy."

Yet, despite his efforts, I sometimes feel so alone in all this. That no matter how much he reaches out, no matter how much he learns, it is I alone who am intimately connected to you. Is that an awful thing to feel? Is it terribly selfish of me to believe that your father can't ever be to you what I already am? Who would have thought how confusing the simple act of bringing a life into the world could be? There is nothing simple about it. I'm torn between terror and excitement, frustration and elation, joy and sorrow. Your poor father looks on in dazed confusion at my constantly drifting state of mind. And the fact is that he's not experiencing this emotional pandemonium, so he can't truly understand it. He wants to, I know, but he just can't. But he's here. He loves us and he's here.

Tonight is New Year's Eve and your daddy and I have decided to make it a quiet one. Calista and Mike got a sitter for Davie and invited us to a party at the Space Needle, where we could dance our way into the New Year, watching the fireworks go off over Elliott Bay, but we told them we felt more like staying home, eating dinner, and maybe watching a movie. What a couple of homebodies we've become. In college we'd be out all night, drinking and dancing until the sun came up. We'd go crazy, be wild. Calista didn't hesitate to point this out to me. "Come *on,* Sarah. The four of us used to go out all the time, and now, the one night I manage to get Mike dressed up and take me dancing, you're staying home? Would you please just get off your butt and go with us? It's going to be a fabulous night." I apologized, but told her staying home with your daddy was my idea of a fabulous time.

Although, with all due respect to your daddy, I do have to say the best New Year's Eve I can remember was spent with Nana Cecille. It was the year my father left. A few weeks after my sixth birthday, I moved in with Nana while your grandmother orchestrated a quick divorce from my daddy and an even quicker marriage to David. They honeymooned in Jamaica over the holidays, sending me some weird voodoo-looking doll for Christmas. When I opened the box and this hideously grinning creature stared back at me, I started to cry. As I hid behind her, Nana held the doll out from her body between pinched fingers. She comforted me, saying the ugly thing made her want to cry too. "Don't worry, peaches," she said. "I'll bury it where it won't ever be found." I don't know if she really buried it, but I never did see that nasty doll again.

Anyway, for New Year's, Nana and I made a huge bowl of popcorn—not the air-popped kind, the kind with oil in a pan. We smothered it in real butter and salt. She let me stay up to watch the Dick Clark special. Of course, I fell asleep far before the ball had dropped in Times Square, but Nana woke me up to count down the last ten seconds. "Come on, peaches," she urged. "Let's go outside and make some noise!"

To this day I will never forget the sight of her, my plump nana in her blue-flowered housedress, skipping through her front yard, waving her fleshy arms around, banging pots and pans with a wooden spoon. She danced and whooped it up, calling up to the sky at the top of her lungs, "Be a fairy, peaches! We can fly! We can be whatever we want, do whatever we want . . . it's a brand-new year! Hap-py New Year, everybody!" I danced along with her, saying I was a fairy, pretending I could fly too, because at that moment I wanted nothing more than to be exactly like the person I loved most in the world.

And tonight the one I love most is in the kitchen. I smell sausage on the grill. He is hard at work on the waffles with blueberry syrup I requested, but I am suddenly craving double chocolate ice cream. We've been hitting Kelly's on a pretty regular basis lately, your daddy's cravings sometimes overwhelming my own. On Monday he managed to down a hot fudge sundae and double dip cone in less than an hour. I've never seen anything like it. Really, though, this sympathy-craving thing is kind of a blast—I don't feel an ounce of guilt for wanting to binge. Ice cream has lots of calcium in it anyway. It's good for you. Well, maybe not *good* for you, but I like to believe it at least nourishes our souls.

Okay. If you can believe it, your daddy just came out of the kitchen to tell me he has a major craving for some Rocky Road. We'll definitely make a run to Kelly's later. At midnight we can toast with ice cream cones instead of champagne flutes. Maybe then we'll go outside to bang some pots and pans. Maybe Nana will hear us.

You are barely three inches long, can you understand what has happened? I certainly cannot. I am lying here. The hospital room is painted an obscenely bright shade of peach. The blinds are drawn tight because I no longer possess any desire to see the light of day. I don't even want to open my eyes. We have lain here together for the past three days, alone.

Your daddy is dead. I don't know any other way to tell you. When we headed out for Kelly's on New Year's Eve, we crossed an intersection and out of nowhere a truck came barreling through a red light and smashed into our car on the driver's side, where your daddy was sitting.

Before I knew that he was dead, I was terrified that you were gone. There was blood between my legs. I got hysterical in the emergency room and they had to give me a sedative. They promised me that the drug would not hurt you. Did you feel it? Did it put you to sleep too?

I woke to find Calista at my bedside, holding my

hand and looking broken. Her usually perky smile was gone, as if someone had taken an eraser and rubbed it across her mouth; her skin was gray and lined. Mike stood behind her, his broad shoulders hunched forward, his chin trembling. Calista wept as she told me Gavin was dead. "The baby is fine, she's fine, but Gavin is gone," she said. She had to say it at least ten times before I could understand the words as they fell from her mouth. He was killed instantly. His neck broken. Snapped to the side. The doctor told me today that your daddy did not understand what was happening to him. That he had no time to think. I disagree. I like to think he thought this: *Sarah. Our baby.*

I'm so sorry. Gavin, my Gavin, your daddy, has left us. My god, the pain. This pain. It is a creature inside me, a thick and roaring monster with claws of sharp steel that dig in and slice my insides to bloody ribbons. I have felt nothing like it in my life. You have to hide from it. You have to curl up tight and hide. Don't let this horror reach you. I don't know how to keep it from you. I breathe in only to feel searing agony in my lungs. I am gasping for the scent of your father. The touch of his hand. The roughness of his beard against the thin skin of my neck. Oh god oh god oh god. It makes no sense. Why? Why why why why why? I can't stop asking why. The only person in my life who loved me without question, without limits, this man, this achingly beautiful man, has been taken from me. Oh god this pain. It is rolling inside me, slamming my heart against my rib cage, bruising the deepest, most sheltered parts of me. The parts only Gavin knew. To see his warm face, to have his hand caress my cheek and the curved, tender spot at the base of my spine. Never, never again. Oh my god he's gone. He's gone. And we are alone.

When Calista first told me, I clapped my hands over my ears. I tried to hit her. I screamed no. "No, no, no! You're lying. Where is he? I want to see him, goddammit. I want to see him now!" I tried to believe in him hard enough to make him not dead. But the dullness in your auntie's eyes, the quiver of Mike's chin, the vise grip of their hands around my wrists, restraining me—this is what convinced me they were telling the truth. Mike tried over and over to speak, but "Oh, god, Sarah, I'm so sorry" was all he could get out before his voice cracked and the tears began to fall.

You and I are not hurt, only a few bruises, but my muscles are aching violently from the tears that are trapped throughout my body. Thousands of tiny tear-shaped stones float along in my blood. The weight of them is staggering, pinning me to this bed, but they refuse to be released. There is a place beyond sadness, a place where tears cannot be shed. I wonder if you feel this paralyzing ache and then I feel worse because I am already causing you pain and I haven't even given birth to you yet. I don't know if I can do this alone. It has always been both your daddy and me, planning to give life to you together. I have no idea how to make it through this without him. He is as much a part of this as you. Something vital is missing and I don't know how I am going to survive. How am I going to live without him? He is your daddy, your father, the one who would hold you with me the minute you are born. Oh god, how am I supposed to do this? Gavin is dead. I keep writing it in the hope I'll understand it. Your father is dead and soon will be burned into ashes. He put it in his will to be cremated; he wants me to bury his ashes in the soil beneath our cherry tree. I don't think I can do it.

It is our fourth day in the hospital, and after Dr. Foster checked in on us this morning, I asked to be taken to see your daddy's body. I had to. I needed proof that he was really gone, that it wasn't just some kind of horrible mistake.

Both Mike and Calista offered to go with me, but I told them no. Mike said he understood, but Calista looked hurt, maybe even a little offended that I didn't want her with me. She is used to being right there, down in the ditches of my crises. "Are you sure, Sarah?" she asked. "It'll be better for you if I'm there. You shouldn't do this alone." She started to reach for the handles of the wheelchair I was sitting in, but I grabbed her wrist. "Calista, no. I don't want you to come. Just stay here." Eyebrows furrowed, she said, "But . . . I don't understand." Something inside me went very cold as I answered her. "You don't have to understand. Just fucking do what I ask you to do, okay?" I was too full of what I was about to do to worry that I might have hurt her.

A nurse wheeled me into the elevator and we went down, down to the hospital's basement and through a long, mint-green hallway to the morgue. Someone brayed like a donkey in the office next to the frigid room where I stood, and I felt the urge to go in and strangle him. Laughter next to the dead is inappropriate. Disrespectful. I told the nurse there should be a rule.

Balancing myself next to the shiny metal tray where he lay, I covered my stomach with both hands to hide your tiny eyes from witnessing your daddy lying still before you. Not breathing. Not moving. Not with us anymore.

He could have been only sleeping if not for the crimson stains smudged across the rice paper of his skin. I held his hand. Touched it to my cheek one last time. It was icy, blue, and stiff. I pushed the black curls from his forehead and gently lifted his eyelids with my thumbs, desperate to see that emerald sparkle once more. "Gavin?" I whispered. "Baby? Can you hear me? Please, please, baby, don't be gone." But his eyes were like fog drifting over the ocean. Clouded and locked, staring blindly ahead. The sparkle had vanished—it followed your father on whatever path he took. I kissed him good-bye. For both of us.

Now we are lying here alone in this hospital room, wires monitoring your heartbeat, right along with mine. They fall in similar patterns; though yours, like a hummingbird's wings, is so much faster. I wonder if my heart is slowing on purpose, willing itself to stop. Dr. Foster came in to see us again this evening. She reassured me that you were going to be okay, that we both will make it through this. "Yeah, okay, whatever, lady," I wanted to say. "You're not knocked up and your husband didn't just fucking die." Instead, I said thank you and I asked her to leave so I could sleep. I could not stand the pity that radiated from her every word. I feel chilled, distant. The tears won't come.

When I asked the nurse for a notepad to write this, I could see that she thought I might be writing a suicide note. She kept insisting I was too tired. "Mrs. Strickland," she said, "you need to get some rest. Just sleep and everything will be better when you wake up." What a fucking idiot. I screamed bloody murder at her—I'm sorry if my anger startled you. I am so heavy with sorrow, and I'm terrified that you are going to leave me too. I need to speak my heart to you, to let you know that I am not going anywhere. There is something fierce within me demanding that I comfort you when I can't even begin to comfort myself.

We left the hospital yesterday, five days after the accident, with orders for bed rest and no undue stress. Some doctor actually wrote that on my chart: "No undue stress." I pointed this out to Calista and asked sharply, "What . . . as if your husband dying is *due* stress?" She looked at me, apprehensive, then patted my head as if to say "Yes, yes, it's all right." She does not know what to do with me.

Shortly before I was scheduled to check out, Calista announced that over the past couple of days she had organized a memorial service for your daddy. "I called about twenty people—they'll be over at your house this afternoon around four o'clock. That place down the street from you guys—you know, that little New York–style deli?—is delivering all the food and stuff at two." Noting the shock on my face, she squeezed my hand. "Don't worry, sweetie, Mike and I will take care of all the cleanup."

I narrowed my eyes, pulled my hand away, and snapped at her. "I'm not worried about the goddamn cleanup, Calista. I just don't think I'm up for dealing with all those people. Why the hell did you plan this without telling me?"

She didn't meet my glance, instead busying herself with the contents of the overnight bag she had brought for me the day after the accident. "I just figured it was better to get it over with. Did you remember to get your toothbrush out of the bathroom?"

I stood up from the bed and snatched my bag from her grasp. "Fuck my toothbrush. Next time you 'figure' something, check with me first, all right?" A wounded look surfaced in her eyes, but she didn't respond. Mike arrived a few minutes later and helped me down to the car while Calista took care of signing me out at the front desk. It was a quiet ride home.

Pretty much everyone Calista had invited showed up. Both Mr. Parkers and all of your daddy's coworkers were there, a few of his clients, along with his Saturday morning basketball buddies. I came out of the bedroom to thank them for coming but could not stay to hear their words of regret, their offers of help and best wishes for your healthy arrival. I felt a little guilty for not sitting with them, but I just couldn't deal with their sympathetic looks, their pitying touches, the whispers floating about the room. I was also furious with Calista and didn't want to be around her. I know I was being selfish, and being selfish is something a woman isn't supposed to do. We're supposed to bend over backward to accommodate everyone else's needs. I could feel how much they needed me to say "Oh, yes, I'll be fine . . . thank you so much . . . oh, yes, just your being here makes me feel so much better . . ." Well, screw that. While they all sat together in our living room, sipping coffee and murmuring in low tones about the tragedy of Gavin's death, I did what *I* needed to do. I curled deep on the bed, my face smothered in your daddy's bath towel. It was sour from days of unwash. No matter how many times I reminded him to do it, he was terrible about remembering to get a fresh towel out of the linen closet. He would use the same towel for a week, until it became unbearable to be in the same room with the rancid thing. I always ended up changing it myself, holding my nose as I threw it into the hamper, silently cursing your daddy for his mindlessness. But yesterday I lay there, grateful I was too lazy to do the laundry last week.

After a few hours everyone except Calista and Mike left. I stayed in bed, listening to the quiet whisper of their voices and the clinking of our best dishes as they straightened the house. I heard Mike ask Calista where to put all the gifts of food people had brought, and then felt his lumbering footsteps come down the hall, pausing outside my door. He didn't knock, but stood there, silent. I could feel him wish that there was something he could do. But there is nothing anyone can do. All I want is to die. If your daddy had to die, I should have died with him. That would have made more sense than leaving me behind. He abandoned me. He abandoned us both.

I went to soak in a scalding tub, hoping the steam would open my pores and somehow this aching sadness would drain out of me. I held one of your daddy's razors to my wrist. Planning to slice down, not across, my veins. Then Calista knocked on the door and I hid the razor underneath the melting bar of soap on the edge of the tub. I got out and she dried me as I stood shivering, not from cold, but from the horror I felt at the thoughts that were racing through my mind.

She gently brushed the tangles from my wet head. "Do you want me to stay with you tonight, sweetie?" My bottom lip convulsed, and unable to speak, I shook my head. "Are you sure?" she asked. "Really, I can stay. I'm going to stay." The compassion in her voice peeled back the fingers of the hard, angry fist that had formed in my chest. "Okay," I managed to whisper.

She guided me to the bed and sat next to me, rubbing my back until Mike came in and whispered to her that he had to get the baby-sitter home before ten o'clock. She walked out into the hall with him, and returning after only a minute, she curled up behind me, her forehead touching my neck, her lips moving against my back. "Do you want to talk?"

I sighed, then said faintly, my voice not sounding like my own, "You know what's strange? It just hit me when you were talking with Mike. I don't have a husband anymore. I'm not somebody's wife. It's just so strange." She pulled me in closer. "I know, sweetie," she said. "I know."

But she's wrong. She doesn't know. She can't know. And for that she should be grateful.

I woke this morning after a few hours of hot, fitful sleep, and for a moment, only a moment, I forgot. I forgot your daddy was gone. I rolled over, reaching for a morning cuddle, and encountered instead a vast, empty expanse. His side of the bed looked barren, a dry and endless white desert; still, I felt as though I were drowning. Gasping for air and then choking on it. Parched, shuddering cries poured silently from my mouth all day long. There are no sounds for this pain.

It feels as though the world is curving in around me, as if I'm trapped in one of those ridiculous dimestore snow globes, only there's no snow. I want to bang on the walls of my new glass universe and demand that I be let back into the real world, the world where my husband is still alive, the world where people are smarter than to get behind the wheel of a car when they are drunk. I want to pound and pound so that somebody will hear me and come rescue me from this nightmare. But it's as though I'm in a dream, flailing and fighting with the full force of my strength, and still, I can't find my target.

Everything is muffled. The phone rings, but it sounds a thousand miles away. Calista's voice is like a fly buzzing next to my ear, and I keep having to ask her to repeat whatever it is she says. Nothing is clear. I feel as if I'm made of the finest blown glass, paper thin, and if anything touches me, I will instantly shatter into a million sharp and jagged pieces. I don't even feel pregnant anymore, although I know you are still within me.

Today, at my request, Calista tracked down your grandmother in Sydney. "I'm not sure of the hotel," I said. "Check my e-mail. She probably left a number." I wanted to talk with my mother, thinking maybe, just maybe, in this one instance, she might possibly be of some help. "I miss him so much," I said quietly. "I'm scared about having the baby without him." Your grandmother cleared her throat. "Sarah, really. You're not actually thinking of keeping this baby, are you? How could you possibly do it? Who will take care of you?"

So much for motherly comfort. I took a deep breath to steady my voice before I responded. "Well. That's just great. Glad to know my own mother believes in me. You know what I'm thinking? I'm thinking you probably shouldn't bother calling anymore if that's how you really feel." I tried to sound angry, sure of myself, though her words tore through me like a knife, deflating any small bubble of confidence that might have existed within me.

"Sarah, I'm thinking of what's best for you. Best

for that child. Do you want your baby growing up poor?" Her voice was hard, demanding.

"Not if growing up poor makes her turn out anything like you," I said coldly, then hung up the phone before she could answer. At that moment, if she had been standing in front of me, I could have slapped her.

Later Dr. Foster called, offering the quiet advice to just keep breathing. She is concerned about us. Concerned this might be too much for you. She wants me to come in every week instead of once a month so she can better monitor us, to make sure the fire of my grief doesn't harm you.

Oh, baby, my baby, please hide from the terror that grips every muscle in my body. Mommy doesn't know how to save you. Hold on, baby. Hold on.

It is so quiet in our house. Too quiet to ever sleep again. Your father was such a noisy man. The way he stumbled to the bathroom in the middle of the night was loud enough to wake the dead. (What a useless analogy—I just realized. There is no way to wake the dead; I know, I have been trying.) All the way down the hall, I could hear him pee. His idea of whispering consisted of leaning in close to me and blowing out my eardrum; he believed his leaning-in covered the secrecy part. I miss the obnoxious way he would chomp his cereal, how he'd slurp his coffee or soup no matter how tepid and drinkable the liquid was. I miss his stale, air-cracking farts. The stupid songs he sang to me at the top of his lungs, the ones he'd make up as he'd go along. It helped him remember our life, singing songs about the everyday things we did together. I wish I had paid more attention to his silly compositions; I cannot remember one thing about them other than that they made me laugh until my stomach felt bruised. God, I miss laughing with him.

Calista stayed with me round the clock the week after the memorial, but this week is here only during the days, leaving Davie with a sitter. We sit in the living room, and I try to smile with her, to pull myself up out of the darkness that surrounds me, but it is a chore. She tells me shiny, meaningless stories about her trips to the market and how the traffic jams through the downtown corridor make it impossible for Mike to get home before seven o'clock. "There was a great deal on tuna fish, so I bought you half a dozen cans—the protein is so good for the baby. I put them in the cupboard above the stove, over on the left-hand side . . . is that okay?" I respond appropriately to her questions, but I just want to shake her. "I don't care, Calista. I don't care," I want to say. "Stop talking. Just shut up and leave me alone." She wants me to act like everything is all right. If I just ignore the pain, it will go away. What she doesn't understand is that this kind of pain is impossible to ignore; it is loud, insistent, constantly present—there is no way to mask it. I know she means well with all her cheery behavior, but still. She needs to give it a rest.

At night, after Calista leaves and the world is lost to the luxury of sleep, I am brightly conscious. I have started going through each room, touching all that was his, and finally, finally, sobbing from somewhere deep inside me. There is something ancient about the tears that rise up through the muscles in my throat and pour out of me, as if they have been long-simmering in some hidden well of anguish—a black and thick bottomless pit of despair waiting to be plumbed. It chokes me, this bubbling and steaming pain. It's like being skinned alive, from the inside out. The sensation pulls and pokes at me like an impatient child desperate for attention, when all I want is to be left alone, wrapped somehow in a blissful state of numbness.

I'm trying to focus entirely on what you need from me, but I am having trouble eating; nothing sounds appealing, and even the chocolate that Mike brought over tonight after Calista went home felt like sawdust against my tongue. He opened his arms to me, pulling me in close; the strength in his embrace conjuring up a fresh ache for my husband. "I miss him too, Sarah," he said. "It'll be okay, I promise. Everything's going to be okay." The words came awkwardly, as though he were trying to convince himself more than me. He disposed of the limp floral arrangements that had turned our living room into a temporary rain forest. As I sat on the sofa beneath a blanket, staring into space, he puttered around, tightening loose cabinet handles, asking me again and again if there was anything else he could do. I finally asked him to put a message on voice mail for my clients, informing them that I had experienced a family tragedy and wouldn't be returning to work anytime soon. A family tragedy. What a neat summation of what has happened. The day I came home from the hospital, Calista called a publicist I know from another agency to cover my workload until I can take over again, but my clients have continued to call me. Strange how the music will play on without me. My clients will go on appearing at clubs, singing and laughing and writing new songs. And your daddy will still be dead and I will be here, barely alive.

This is what I do: I cling to your father's picture. I wrap my arms tight around my body, thinking this might somehow keep me from falling apart. I bargain with God. I promise Him that if I can have your daddy back, I will start going to church. I will volunteer my time to work with needy families, and every week I will tithe not just ten but twenty percent. If I can have your daddy back, I will never say *fuck* again. I will retrain my nasty tongue to sing hymns and murmur prayers and proclaim God's glory.

I don't think God is listening.

I know I'm selfish. You must be feeling this turmoil—are you enduring? I wish I could make it all go away. My mother's voice plays over and over in the back of my mind: "How can you possibly do it? Who's going to take care of you?" A wicked recording that has no end.

At my first checkup outside the hospital since the accident, I sat cold and half naked in Dr. Foster's exam room, weeping softly as I told her that I didn't know if

I would be able to go through with having you. "Of course, it's your decision," she said. "But fifteen weeks is pretty far along to terminate a pregnancy." The muscles in my stomach contracted violently at the sound of the word *terminate*. She continued, "If you want, I can give you the number of someone to talk to, someone who specializes in counseling women with this kind of issue." She reached out to me, cradling both my hands in her own. "Sarah, I know how much this baby meant to both you and Gavin. You're in so much pain right now . . . not the best place to make a decision as big as this one. Think hard, okay?"

It was later that night, and I was on the phone with Calista when she reminded me that you, my sweet baby, are by and large the only remainder of Gavin. "It's like he gave you the gift of himself, Sarah. Do you really want to say no to that?" I fingered the charm your daddy gave me on Christmas; it hadn't left my neck since that morning, and I know now that I will never take it off. Calista was right: You are carrying your father's sweet and gentle nature in your blood. His humor in your veins. You might have his eyes, his brilliant green eyes. What is precious to me, no—what *was* precious to me about him might be found in you. This realization has renewed my determination to handle this grief. I think it's probably what kept the razor from digging into my flesh. I don't know how I will do this, just that somehow I will.

The clouds piled upon one another this cold January afternoon, layered like rough mounds of steel wool bulging with the threat of rain. I was sitting on the couch, staring out the window to the darkened sky, looking for some sign that there might be a heaven, when Calista came by to drop off a stack of books on the grieving process. She set them on my lap, saying, "I thought these'd be good for you to have around. Maybe give you some ideas on what you can do to make yourself feel better."

I looked through the titles, as foreign to me as if they had been printed in Chinese. The letters blurred before me. "Take them back," I whispered hoarsely, pushing them toward her. "I don't want them here." She drew a circle on my back with the soft touch of her hand. "Sweetie, I know it's hard. You don't have to read them all right now. I just thought . . . if you had questions or thoughts or fears . . . you know, you might find them helpful. I'll put them on the nightstand in your room, okay? Just in case. Then I've got to get going . . . Davie's sitter can only be with him till four today.''

Silent, I watched her go down the hall to the bedroom, then out the front door. I could not explain to her how just the thought of all those words, the horrifying content of the stories within those pages, made me feel as if I were standing ankle-deep in cement, immobile, about to be flattened by an oncoming bus. I could not explain to her how it has been almost a month since the accident and I still believe if I stare at the door long enough, your daddy will walk through it. There is no way to explain any of this.

I miss your daddy so much. His hot skin next to mine at night, my own personal furnace. The nightly collision of our limbs, the stink of his breath after he made love to me with his tongue.

I want him back. Goddammit. I want him back.

Last night I drove. I drove and drove with no particular destination in mind; I knew only that I had to get away from the house. Our house. Your father is everywhere: in the paint, in the windows, in the bathroom. I sit on the toilet and see his razor tilted against the soap dish. I stand in front of the kitchen sink, and there on the windowsill is his coffee mug, the one I got him two years ago for Christmas that proclaims MEAN PEOPLE SUCK BUT NICE PEOPLE SWALLOW. He chuckled at the phrase every morning. I pick up the mug and press the edge to my mouth, working my lips against its rim in a delirious attempt to feel his kiss again. In the living room there is the shadow of him in the dent of the couch, where he sat to read, to eat, to watch "The Three Stooges". He loved Moe. "Moe is their leader," he'd say, mimicking the goofy tone of Homer Simpson, a cartoon character from another one of his favorite shows. Your father had such a fabulous sense of humor, completely offbeat and terribly sarcastic. He was a fantastic smart-ass, but not everybody got him at first. We'd be at a party and he'd make some offhand comment and new acquaintances would look at him like "*What? Is he serious? What the hell is he talking about?*" And there I'd be, on the floor, hysterical. I got him. I got him better than anyone else in this world ever did. And now I don't have him anymore.

Did you hear me howl? Did it make you cry too? That's a good thing about the car; you can howl and howl and nobody can hear you. You should try to remember that. There is barely a soul on the street at three A.M., no one to look at you strangely as your face twists into a grimace of undefinable despair.

I ended up in a strip mall parking lot, somewhere past Sea-Tac Airport, not remembering how I got there. Truly. I could not recall, for the life of me, getting into the car and driving. I remember only the howling. My eyes were swollen into hot little slits. I rubbed you; over and over I let my hand move across the bare skin of my rounded belly. I was trying to touch you. God, I'm going to be a terrible mother. How selfish I am. I'm trying, I swear I'm trying, but this is killing me. I'm not sure if I can make it through. But I have to. Another thing I must do—I must save you from me. I'll just add it to the list. You don't deserve any of this, I know. How must this be for you? Are you terrified? Are you floating around, thrashing against me in a struggle to escape the pain I am bleeding into you? What kind of mother am I?

Dr. Foster told me this week that I need to monitor my stress levels better and stay calm in the midst of this chaos. Right. Easy for her to say. She ordered me to do deep breathing to keep from exploding from the pressure that is building inside me. She also suggested that four months along in the pregnancy was a good time to get signed up for prenatal classes. "No," I said sharply, then attempted to quiet my tone. "I mean, I can't handle the idea of being around all those happy expecting couples. There is no way I can keep repeating 'My husband is dead' as an explanation for his absence." She nodded. "Okay. Sure. I understand. But what about going with a friend, like Calista? Lots of women choose that option."

I thought about it for a few minutes but at some gut level knew that going to those classes with Calista would only further the strain I've felt building between us. She might see my asking her to come with me as a sign that I'm willing to pretend everything is normal, that I'm ready to forge ahead—using breathing patterns and relaxation techniques as a means to distract me from my grief. Part of my reluctance, too, I suppose, is related to how protective I feel of you right now. I don't want to share you with anybody, not even Calista. I feel like taking those classes with her would be letting her in too close, like I'd be inserting her in the place your daddy was supposed to be. Replacing him. "I just can't," I told Dr. Foster. "It just wouldn't work for me right now. Is there any way I can learn the breathing on my own? Can you give me some things to read?"

She rifled around in her desk for a minute, then offered me a stack of pamphlets and promised to send more over to the house so I can educate myself. "Let me know if you have any questions," she said. "And I'm going to quiz you to make sure you are learning what you need to, okay? Don't forget to keep breathing."

When I got home, I took all your daddy's clothes out of the closet, laid them on the bed, and rolled around naked in them. I wrapped myself in the smell of him, practicing my new breathing exercises with a vengeance so that you could acquaint yourself with him. Did it get through to you, his warm scent of sweat and sandalwood? He never wore cologne; I told him that he didn't have to, that his natural scent of damp soil and sweet wood-smoke was fragrant enough.

Later that night Calista and I were sitting at the kitchen table, and I said, "You know what? If I had known I would lose him, I would have gone to one of those specialty shops in the mall—you know, the ones where you can have them concoct a personalized scent?—and create the smell of Gavin's skin. Then, whenever I wanted, I could spread it all over me. I could put it behind my ears and between my breasts and at the pulse points on my wrists and the back of my knees, and it would be as if he had been there, rubbing himself against me." Tears filled her eyes. "Oh, sweetie," she said. "I'm so sorry." She keeps telling me she's sorry. Sometimes I wish she'd just keep her damn mouth shut. It would do as much good. God, I sound angry. I don't mean to. It just keeps coming.

Tonight I rubbed your daddy's worn fleece sweat pants against my bulging belly. I want so much for you to know him, to experience the extraordinary person who helped create you. I know we weren't perfect, but I have to say that God is just plain fucking vicious to make me lose him. In fact, I'm starting to doubt His existence, even more so than I did before. Well-meaning acquaintances have sent notes that claim a higher purpose for Gavin's death, a plan that God has laid out for all of our lives. Well, I'm sorry, but I can't see any kind of good coming from a plan that takes a beautiful man away from his wife and unborn child. There isn't any fucking plan. Horrible, devastating things just happen. And if there were a God, a truly merciful and protective deity, He would prevent them.

Calista doesn't believe in God, but she has tried to tell me that things happen for a reason. "Maybe good people die young so the purity of their spirit can contribute to the positive energy flow of the universe. Maybe Gavin's soul is battling evil." Your auntie is a bit out there. She is all into the karma of life, the never-ending circle of it all. I am to a certain point in agreement with her. But she is not the one who has lost her husband. Despite all their problems, she still has Mike's furry chest to nuzzle into with the tip of her nose when she climbs in bed at night; Mike to bring her chicken soup when she has the flu and can't move from the couch; Mike to hold hands with for a midnight stroll in the park; Mike to press her naked body against and have the knot between her thighs gently untwined by his fingers. I want her to stop telling me it is a matter of time. Time may help, but right now, in this particular moment of horror, knowing time will help does about as much good for me as an ice maker would do for an Eskimo. A client of mine sent a sympathy card that proclaimed whatever doesn't kill you makes you stronger. What a crock. Who comes up with that shit?

Another day spent wandering the house, picking things up, not seeing them or feeling their presence in my hands, then setting them back down, usually in the wrong place. I found a frying pan in the bathtub this morning, and yesterday, a pair of my underwear in the silverware drawer.

If only we could go back and not want ice cream to celebrate the New Year. If only we had bought some earlier that day. If only we had taken the long way to Kelly's. If only your daddy had taken longer putting on his shoes and we had left five minutes later. If only I could have died with him.

As Calista sat with me today, I told her I feel like I'm searching for the rewind button in my life. But there's no remote control, no magic button that will go back frame by frame, editing out the death scene because it turns out to be too much for the audience to handle.

I'm not showering. I'm oily, my forehead has become a topographical map of angry red, pus-filled zits.

My appetite has resurfaced with a vengeance; every chocolate cake and tuna casserole left in the freezer from the memorial has been annihilated. At my checkup with Dr. Foster this morning, I found out I'm up twenty pounds—twice what I'm supposed to have gained at seventeen weeks into the pregnancy. I can't stop putting food into my mouth. I'm not looking in the mirror. I am sitting at the kitchen table, staring at the grain of the wood until it takes on a life of its own, squirming and vibrating before me. Hours pass. My heart's insistence to continue beating is astonishing.

I'm out of clean clothes. I tried to do a load of wash, but for the life of me, I could not remember how to make the machine work. Do I put the clothes in first, or the detergent? Do whites mix with pink? Can I wash jeans with a cream silk blouse? The whole ordeal reduced me to tears. I spent the rest of the day on the floor of the utility room, clutching my dirty underwear and listening for the intermittent hum of the refrigerator on the other side of the wall.

How am I going to survive this? How are you going to survive me? God, I'm so sorry this is happening. Sleep. I just want to sleep.

I was in your nursery tonight after Mike and Calista had gone home, once again wide awake. It was so quiet. It's amazing, the silence of midnight—the whole world seems frozen. Moonlight oozed like spilled oil over the wood floor, and I stood looking out the window up to the stars, wishing hard upon them for this all to be a dream. That I would wake up and your father would be there to hold me close in our bed, rocking me in his arms, kissing that magic spot behind my left ear. I looked out to the cherry tree, a fragile silver shadow against the velvet backdrop of the night sky, and I wondered how I was ever going to work up the courage to bury your father there. Weariness spun itself like a web around me, and for a moment I closed my eyes.

It was then that I felt him. I felt your father all around me as if the night air were the breath from his lungs and he had just pursed his lips and whistled softly against my skin. When I lifted my eyes back to the tree, he was there, in the clothes he was wearing our last night together, jeans and a green T-shirt. His hands were shoved into his front pockets as usual, and he kicked at the dirt with his bare right foot. I wondered what happened to his shoes. I thought, Maybe you don't need shoes in heaven. And then, Wait, I don't believe in heaven. And finally, Who gives a shit about his shoes? I dashed through the house and out the back door, my hands clapped over my mouth. Small squeaking sounds popped out of me. He grinned and walked slowly toward me. I couldn't say a word. He didn't look like a ghost, I couldn't see through him. There weren't any bruises on his skin, and the light still shimmered in his eyes. He was alive. The accident hadn't happened. There had been some kind of mistake. I rushed over to meet him.

He held me. Solid flesh, he was, I swear to you. I felt the warmth of his skin, I breathed him in. I bore my gaze into his eyes, and though his mouth did not move, I heard his voice in my head, whispering to me that everything would be all right, that he is watching over us. Then this: *Believe in me, Sarah . . . believe that I'm here with you,* and he started to drift away. I grabbed his face and told him to stay, that he couldn't leave. I begged him, got down on my knees and gripped my arms around his legs so that he couldn't walk away. It did nothing to restrain him. He leaned down to caress you through my belly with such tenderness, such awe, and the look that passed between us reached in, took my heart right out of my chest and twisted it violently, like a wet rag. And as suddenly as he had appeared, he was gone.

I don't know if I imagined this happening. I keep getting up from writing this and looking out the window to the tree, just in case he has returned and is waiting for me. Maybe I'm just crazy. I *feel* crazy. My god, but how real he was. How wonderful he smelled, and when I looked in his eyes, I saw everything I know he would have said to me if he had lived long enough to say good-bye. How much he loves me. How much he loves us both. And yet it's still not good enough. I want him back, not just in a dream or a hallucination or whatever the hell tonight was. I want to dig my nails into his back and press him to me. God, oh, god, what the hell am I going to do?

A Jehovah's Witness came to the door this morning, preaching to me about God's love and understanding and forgiveness. I told him to fuck off and slammed the door in his face. I have never been so bitchy in all my life. It's like I'm watching a movie of myself: the fat pregnant lady with the dead husband who is having hallucinations and steadily going crazy, one irrational moment after the next.

Am I feeding you enough? I want to eat lots of salad and whole grain bread, but it's just not happening. So much for my nutritious eating plan. I really was going to feed you better—I had a shopping list of vegetables and protein all set up on the computer to print out each week, but here I am, six weeks into my second trimester, and I'm letting every green leafy item Calista puts in the fridge go brown and slimy. I never craved cookies and candy bars this much before I got pregnant, which makes me think you're the one demanding them. If I ever had doubts about my ability to be a good mother, I am having them now. I mean, really. I can't even say no to a fetus.

This afternoon I stood at the kitchen window, eating a bowl of chocolate pudding with a fork because I couldn't find any clean spoons, when a bright yellow moving truck rumbled up the street to the house next door. At ninety-six, our old neighbor, Mr. Winchester, finally agreed to move into a nursing home this past summer and ever since, a lonely FOR SALE sign has been stabbed in the front lawn. I hadn't noticed the real estate agent showing the house, but a few days ago the sign disappeared, and today a cherry-red Mustang convertible with California license plates pulled up behind the truck. A tall, slender blonde popped out of the driver's seat, her long, tan legs and flat stomach immediately pissing me off. She arched her back and stretched, her perky tits pointing even farther up than they already had a right to. She proceeded to tilt her head flirtatiously at the movers, gesturing with perfectly manicured fingertips where to set her belongings. She hopped—really, she actually *hopped*—clapped her hands, then ran excitedly up the front steps of her new home. The movers carried in what looked like a dining room set right out of *House Beautiful*. After seeing the brass bed I've always wanted but never have been able to afford, I knew I was going to hate this woman. I retreated to bed with my pudding and a bag of Oreos.

I know, we're spending way too much time in bed, watching mindless television. I'm sorry for exposing you to the nonsense of daytime programming, but it allows my mind to flee into a different world, far away from the one in which we live. I get so angry at the stupid characters on the soaps, I actually throw the remote at the screen to get their attention. I'm seething—the fury that fills me is like iron; it is my anchor. I don't know what I'm so pissed about. I want to be only sad. Quiet, solemn bereavement seems more appropriate for a woman who has lost her husband. But instead, I waver between wanting to punch holes in the wall and wanting to collapse to the floor and curl fetal. The pressure inside me is thick and debilitating and hopeless. It feels as though it will never end.

This afternoon I told Calista about the fantasies I'm having of hunting down and strangling the man who drove his truck into us. I told her I want to dig my fingers into the flesh of his neck and see his tongue pop out between his swollen blue lips and watch as the life drains out of his eyes. I want to hear the rattle of his last breath, to know I'm responsible for making him pay in full for the atrocity he committed.

"You know what I think?" she said after hearing me say this. "I think it might be a good idea for you to start trying to work through some of that anger. Beat up a pillow or something. Pretend it's the bastard and beat the shit out of him." When I told her there weren't enough pillows in the world to endure the anger I feel, she shrugged. "Well, you need to do something with all those nasty feelings . . . it's not healthy to hold them in." My laugh came out as a short, dry bark. "*Excuse* me?" She looked genuinely surprised. "What?"

"Oh, come *on*. You've been known to push down

a feeling or two." She was quiet for a minute, fiddling with the mug she held in her hands. Then, as she quickly changed the course of the conversation to some cute thing Davie had said the night before, I realized I didn't have it in me to pursue the subject.

After Calista went home, I thought about whether —if presented with the opportunity—I'd actually hurt the man who hit us. If he walked through this door right now, I might. Who knows? The bastard is out on bail, waiting for a sentencing hearing. The prosecuting attorney called and told me the jerk is going to plead guilty but that I shouldn't hold out too much hope for a long jail sentence. "It's only his first drunk driving offense," she said. I don't really give a fuck. He killed my husband, your father, and he should pay. And for some stupid reason, our legal system won't give him what he deserves; they'll give him a second chance. What a backwards world we live in. If I decided right now to go out and kill him, I would probably go to prison for the rest of my life because I willfully chose to take his life. But he can argue that what he did was an accident; he was drunk, he had no idea what he was doing. That he isn't responsible. Which I think is complete bullshit. He willfully drank himself into a stupor, willfully did not take a taxi, willfully got behind the wheel of his truck—a two-ton killing machine—and willfully rammed into us, murdering your daddy. I can't believe the rage I feel toward this person, this man I've never even met. Before now, I don't think I've ever truly wished somebody dead.

I'm just so afraid of being alone. There's an emptiness surrounding me, a loss so expansive I can't even

begin to name it. Wherever there is an object gone, I
see your father. I'm hurting from someplace below my
stomach, right where you are. Is this your pain? Do
you even know what I'm going through? This tight,
hot, pulsing crimson pain? God, I feel so completely
overwhelmed. I'm sliding down a slippery slope into
this horrifying, impenetrable darkness and I don't
know how to stop. There are no roots to grab hold of,
no cushion to break my fall. My heart is a solid stone
inside my chest; it is a labor to take a breath. Yesterday
I stayed under the covers all day long, getting up only
to pee on your demand, when what I really need to do
is pay bills and go grocery shopping and get your
daddy's car fixed. No, I'm going to sell his car. I can't
ever look at it again. Calista will take care of it for me.

I know women have children and raise them as
single mothers every day. I do not want to be one of
those women. I don't want to put you in daycare, but
how am I going to make a living and look after you?
I'm draining our savings every day I don't work—the
few residual checks that have come in were spent on
the cremation and two months' house payments.
What about health insurance? I've got to call your
daddy's office and ask if we are still covered, at least for
the duration of this pregnancy. I'll see if Calista can
take care of that too.

I think there may be some life insurance money
that will tide us over. But how am I going to make the
house payments for the next twenty years? Please,
baby, don't you worry. Please, just be strong and grow
and be healthy. Your mommy will take care of you, I
just miss your father so much. I can do this, I just
might need a little time. How soon you will be here.

Will you ask for your daddy? Will you see other little girls with their daddies and feel as though you are missing something? How many times will you want to know why your daddy had to leave us? How in the hell will I answer you?

Calista and Mike got a sitter for Davie a few nights ago and came over to fix me dinner. I practically burst right open from the envy that rose up within me. I cannot stand to see them together anymore. The careless way Calista ignores Mike's hand at the small of her back, his ignorance of the adoration that shines in her eyes for him. I want to shake Calista, to say "Goddammit . . . *look* at what you have. Take a minute and be thankful for every second you share with this person. Don't take him for granted. Pay attention. Do whatever it takes to fix what's broken between you. Do it now. Don't wait. Don't you understand? It all can be gone in an instant."

Being around them that night, I felt a jealousy push through me, a jealousy so hard and heavy, it flattened my heart. Does this mean that I am jaded? I'm only twenty-eight and I'm already jaded. The love of my life is gone. I suppose I should be thankful that another is on the way, due out from inside my body in only four and a half months.

I was sitting on the living room floor today with the shades drawn tight, hugging your daddy's pillow and trying to find a reason to take a shower, when I heard the roar of a lawn mower in our front yard. I leapt to the window, believing with everything in me that I would see your father in his ripped-out blue jeans pushing the machine across the grass. I swear, I believed it, and when my eyes found only Richard, our neighbor from across the street, I broke down. Simply crumpled to the floor and wept. He was out there for hours in the middle of an unseasonably dry and warm February day, mowing and edging our yard, pulling limp horsetails and dandelions from beneath the rhododendrons, trimming back the rosebushes I planted last spring, and all I could do was sob.

It's amazing to me how people try, in their own ways, to help out where they can. Richard and your daddy never got along very well; the conflict came from something between men that I didn't understand and your father couldn't explain to me. They nodded briskly to each other if their paths ever crossed, and Richard has never spoken more than a "good morning" to me. He isn't the type of neighbor we invited to our summer barbecues—he is always working, dressed sharply in three-piece suits and spit-shined shoes. We always figured he was a lawyer or a stockbroker but never got far enough in a conversation to ask. In the wee hours between midnight and morning, I have sometimes seen him escort a willowy redhead through his front door, but he lives alone. It never even crossed my mind that he might be lonely. How wrapped up in our own worlds we become. I didn't realize that he even knew Gavin was gone. He must have seen all the people at the memorial service and drawn his own conclusions. Or maybe he has just heard me cry out in the night. How wonderful of him to make such a gesture, to take care of a task that at the moment is insurmountable for me. To not even ask, to just do it. People show their goodness in odd ways. It reminded me to look for the good. It's always in there, somewhere.

After Richard went home, I went out in the backyard to the cherry tree. When I stand beneath its branches, the world that has become so peripheral, so blurred and gray around me, suddenly falls clear again, as if all that is broken and disjointed within me is blessed by some healing touch. Sometimes your daddy is there, sitting next to me, even though he does not speak. Do you think that your mother is losing her mind? She thinks that she might be, and for that reason I don't reach out to him anymore, for fear that my hand will find only the empty air and confirm my suspicion that I'm imagining things; I choose instead to let my eyes simply drink in his image.

Today I watched as your daddy sat next to me and ran his fingers through the damp, newly cut grass, then raised his hand to his face in order to breathe the sweet scent in. I said nothing, only looked on in amazement as he smiled at me, urging me with the sparkle of his eyes to copy his actions, and so I did—I rubbed my fingers against the ground, then sucked the juicy bouquet into my lungs. I wondered if you could smell it yet. If you could, that is what green smells like.

We stayed beneath that tree, your father and I, and I talked to him, telling him the stories of my heart until dusk settled its lavender netting around us and my belly began to rumble, the pesky reminder of my need to eat. I think I'd be content to stay beneath that tree every minute of the day if it meant I could be with him. But he does not always appear to me, which is what makes me doubt whether I really ever see him at all.

But then, later, I remembered once coming upon Nana Cecille as she sat in her kitchen, shelling sugar snap peas from the garden. She was talking to the chair next to her as though something more than air were sitting in it. "What are you doing, Nana?" I asked. "Who are you talking to?" She pulled me to her lap, kissed my ear, and fed me a sweet, crunchy pea. "Oh, I was just talking things over with your grandpa." I screwed up my face and said, "Grandpa? You can't talk to Grandpa. He's dead." She laughed. "Yes, my peaches. I know that. But he lived in this house a long, long time, so when I need him, he comes to visit. We have a little chat and catch up on things. Now, get busy and help me finish with these peas. We've got canning to do."

At the time I didn't really grasp what she meant about being able to see and talk to my dead grandpa. Now I believe maybe I do. Maybe, just maybe, your daddy's image is not a hallucination. Perhaps, instead, it is simply the reflection of my heart, in such deep need of him.

I actually worked up the courage to walk to the grocery store today. I have decided that I can't rely on Calista to do my shopping for me forever. In a little over four months, I'm going to be responsible for a whole other life besides my own, so I feel like I'd better at least make an effort to be self-sufficient again. It's been way too easy laying all of life's everyday tasks on Calista; she's so eager to do anything that will bring me back to normal, I've probably taken advantage of her. And anyway, she can't take care of me like this forever—she has her own family to deal with. Plus, her cheerfulness when she scrubs my toilet or puts away the groceries makes me want to run screaming from the room. "Oh, yes," part of me wants to say, "let's be happy about a bargain on oatmeal and that lemon-fresh scent, even though my husband just died and I'm about to be a single mother." Her Little Mary Sunshine routine is getting old.

I took no shower before I left for the store, wore no makeup—it was just me and my greasy hair and

Gavin's purple sweat pants. I took the long way, criss-crossing through the side streets instead of going straight down Queen Anne Avenue, in order to avoid the intersection where the accident happened. I am definitely not ready to look at that spot yet. In fact, I'm slightly terrified that I will dash into the street and let the cars smash me as they may. At the moment, self-control is not my strongest virtue.

I carried a list with three items written on it: milk, prunes, and bran. All the junk food I've been eating is stopping me up like nobody's business. My shit is rock solid, sharp and painful to pass. Dr. Foster told me I've got hemorrhoids, so I need to bulk up on the fiber. Jesus. Nobody tells you what this pregnancy thing really does to your body. Bright red stretch marks are starting to tear up the skin across my newly protruding belly. I rub more and more cream into them every day, but they just keep getting worse. I feel huge. My center of gravity is completely off balance; even as I stand still, I sway around and around and side to side. I'm moving, but it's like wading through Jell-O. Grape Jell-O, dark and thick around me, slowing my movements and suffocating my every breath. Even my teeth ache; are you sucking the calcium right out of them?

When I got to the store, a man in the produce department hit on me. I just couldn't believe it. There I stood, fat and greasy and smelly as a pig, and this grocery clerk came up to me. Right next to the tomatoes. "You sure you know how to pick out a good one?" He winked at me. I nodded. "Got it under control? You sure? 'Cause I could show you how to press a tomato just right to check for the correct ripeness, if you wanted me to. There's a science to it, you know. Got to have the right amount of pressure and release to make sure you're getting a good one."

I looked him over: He was young, about my age —maybe a few years younger even—with wild yellow hair that twisted out from his scalp. It wanted to get away from him too. I wanted to ask him if his eyes were made of ice. He was handsome, I guess, in a childlike sort of way, but I only glared at his ridiculously hopeful grin. "Do you mind?" I said. "I'm trying to shop in peace." He held his hands up, palms open. "Sorry, just trying to be friendly." I smirked. "Yeah, right, I know what you're trying to do. My husband just died and I'm pregnant, all right? So go fuck yourself."

I suppose I was a little rough on him. How could he have known? But I didn't care. I wanted to dig my fingernails into his eyeballs and tear them to shreds so he could have just a taste of how I'm feeling. "See?" I would have shrieked. "See? This is how it is! Do you want to get laid now?" Fuck. My tongue feels thick in my mouth as I write this. My insides are swelling from the pain. I'm going to explode.

I have to stop this right now. I have to take care of you. I have to hire a painter to sponge puffy white clouds across the ceiling in your room so you will never feel that you are trapped indoors. I have to stop eating so damn much. I have to wash the stench from between my legs. I have to call my clients and let them know that I'm not dead, only critically ill. I have to start my low-impact pregnancy aerobics. I have to practice my breathing and relaxation techniques. I have to pick out your name. *I have to I have to I have to*. Christ. I still don't think I can do this.

Your daddy came to me again last night as I sat shivering in the backyard, staring blindly up into the blue satin sky. My back was pressed against the rough bark of what I am starting to think of as his tree, and I was trying to convince myself it was time to do the task, to buck up and follow through with his request, to bury his ashes in this spot, when I started to nod off. His hand on my bare foot woke me. *Sarah-bara,* his voice whispered in my head, *who's this sleeping beneath my tree?* I blinked hard, twice, to make sure I wasn't just imagining the pressure of his fingers massaging my toes. Was I dreaming? Perhaps. But then he sat down next to me, his ankles crossed, knees pulled up to his chest, and folded his arms, one forearm over the other. He cupped his elbows with his palms. I wanted to throw myself against him, but I was terrified that trying to touch him would break the magic of this spell. He spoke no more, simply looked at me, expectant. I told him all about you. "She might have some hair on her head now, honey. Do you think she'll have your curls? I hope so. I hope she gets your eyes too. My nose though." I looked at him sideways. "Just kidding, hon. You have a beautiful nose." He continued his silence, so I went on. "Can you believe she's bending to suck her fingers and toes? They're not even all the way formed yet and she wants to suck on them. Dr. Foster says babies do that to practice for breast-feeding."

I babbled for a while longer, but then, after I honestly started to believe he was there, and before I could convince him to stay, he was gone. I think I closed my eyes for only an instant—I was so tired—and when I was startled awake, the air was empty around me. But I could still feel him. All around us. Holding me up as I struggled back into the house, by habit to our bedroom, and then finally, by necessity, to the couch, since it is only getting more difficult to sleep in the bed without him. Too much space. And despite what he says, feeling him in my heart is not the same as having him pressed physically against me. It is not enough.

The doorbell rang just a while ago, a delivery man from the Greek café with a salad of crisp cucumbers and tomatoes, pita bread, and grilled chicken souvlaki. He handed me a card along with the food and wished me congratulations for a healthy baby. I forgot to tip him. The note was from Dr. Foster. "Sarah!" it said. "Eat! It's good, I promise. Take a hot shower, shave your legs, slather yourself with yummy lotion . . . and please, get some sleep. Take good care of yourself, both you and your little sweetie are doing fine. I'll see you next week."

I smiled at her thoughtfulness. That morning, at my five-month checkup, I weighed in at thirty-five pounds heavier than my pre-pregnancy weight. "Oh, my god, I'm a cow!" I cried. Dr. Foster laughed and shook her head. "You are *not* a cow, Sarah. Lots of women gain more than they are supposed to. Food is a good coping substance. Listen, hon, with all you're dealing with, I'm just happy you're not downing bottles of Chianti. If it really bothers you, try upping your exercise." Right, I thought. Upping it from what? Dragging my ass from the couch to the refrigerator?

When I returned home from my appointment, Calista was sitting on the front porch, waiting for me. We went to the kitchen, where she made hot cocoa to go with the chocolate-covered almond biscotti she had baked the night before. My second cookie half gone, I began to cry. Calista stood up and wrapped her arms around me. "Sarah, honey, what's wrong?"

"I shouldn't be eating this," I sobbed. "I'm so fat. I'm disgusting. My underwear is big enough for the both of us. . . ." My shoulders shook at the thought of my enormous white cotton panties.

Calista sat back down, still squeezing my hand, and smiled. "Oh, sweetie, you look just beautiful. I've been meaning to tell you, you've got that pregnant-woman glow, all shiny and peaceful-looking. Really, you look great. Never better." Her compliment quieted my tears; I hadn't realized how much I had missed having someone tell me I was beautiful. That was your daddy's job. It was also a relief to feel connected with Calista—we've been missing the mark with each other so often lately. When she tries to do or say something to make me feel better—like when she brought over those books or when she suggested that I beat up a pillow to deal with my anger—it mostly just irritates me that she's trying to fix something she can't understand. Her saying I am beautiful just the way I am, flabby butt and all, her knowing how it feels to be pregnant and fat and knowing the exact words to say, was even more affirming than she probably realized.

I do wonder if my weight gain would bother your

dad. It's not like I was thin in the first place. I'm pretty average except for my big boobs and bubbled butt. I used to fret all the time about gaining weight, until Gavin just told me to put a sock in it. He said he loved me no matter what, and I should just quit my bitching. But sometimes, only sometimes, I would catch his eyes traveling over my body as I bent over in the shower, my belly scrunching into a fleshy accordion and my breasts sagging like distended water balloons. He didn't have any particular look on his face; I couldn't tell if he was disgusted or enthralled. I also couldn't bring myself to ask. No woman wants to hear her husband say he's repulsed by the new turns her body is taking.

Your daddy was an athlete; he ran every morning and did a hundred sit-ups in front of the eleven o'clock news. He played basketball on Saturdays. I watched admiringly. He tried to get me involved with his active lifestyle, but the honest-to-God truth is I hate exercise. I'd much rather sit and read or watch a good movie than sweat. I know, I know, I need to move my body. If for anything, for you. It was a point of contention between your father and me, little one. I think it bothered him that I wasn't very concerned about my health. I've always kind of figured that you should enjoy what life hands out to you, then, even if you keel over from a cholesterol-stuffed heart, you can say you did what you wanted; you were happy. Funny that he was the health-conscious one and I'm the one living the long life. Funny strange, not funny ha-ha. Someday you'll understand the difference.

I'll be doing fine, better, feeling like I might actually get through the day without crying, when suddenly, without warning, there it is. The pain starts to move again, rising and rising until it crashes against my hope that things might eventually get better, demolishing it, then receding, only to begin its ascent all over again. It's like I'm a piece of driftwood, bobbing along, utterly helpless, at the mercy of the tide, not sure if I will ever reach a safe harbor. Dr. Foster said I should really think about talking to the therapist she's recommended. I don't know. I don't know what good it will do me. Plus I'm afraid it will use up the money I need to save so I can manage to care for you. I also don't know if I could actually tell anyone other than you that your daddy appears to me. But I told her that I would at least think about it.

I was fine today until Calista brought over your father's ashes. Since the memorial, she and Mike have been keeping them for me; I couldn't stand to see them, let alone have them near me. Without even asking if I was ready to have them here with me yet, she brought them over to the house. Seeing the blue box in her hands, knowing what it contained, I was stunned. Absolutely speechless. Uncomfortable with my silence, Calista said almost sheepishly, "Well, I just thought you should have these with you now." When I didn't respond, she hugged my rigid body, then left, saying, "I'll call you later." Shivering, I forced myself to look at the box on the table in front of me. Its surface is etched with your daddy's full name in swirling black italics: Gavin Lee Strickland. Below that the day of his birth and the day of the accident. The day he died.

You know, no matter how many times I say or write or think that your father has died, I still don't really believe it happened. I sit in the living room, cuddled against my usual corner of the couch during the evening news, watching the door, waiting for him to stroll on in. "Sarah, baby!" he'd say. "Say hello to your storm trooper of love!" I imagine him wrapping me up in his thick arms and shoveling his scratchy face into my neck. He shaved only every other day. "Give us a kiss, hot mama. Some of that mondo good lovin'!" His grin, his Chiclet grin. "My, what big teeth you have!" I'd croon in mock horror. "The better to eat you with, my dear," he'd growl. Oh god. A little part of me believes that if I just do everything the same as I used to, be there in the exact spot he always found me in, he'll come back. If I lay out his shoes, he will come fill them. If I play the hideous music he loved, he'll burst through a door, vigorously strumming an air guitar. If, if, if.

I pick up the phone to call him at least six times a

day. The receiver is to my ear and the number to his office half dialed before I remember that there is nobody at his desk, that one of the Mr. Parkers had his secretary call the other day to ask when I was coming to clean it out and take down our pictures.

But now, thanks to Calista, his burnt-up body is sitting on the coffee table. What the hell does she know about grief that makes her think she can decide when I should be done with mine? After the other morning when we shared that brief connection over my feeling so fat, I had thought things might start getting better between us, but I see now the distance between us is growing. If she had even the slightest idea of what I'm going through, she would have kept your daddy's ashes until I asked for them. It must be driving her crazy that she can't "fix" me like she "fixes" herself. I know I need to say something to her, but I am having the hardest time taking care of my own shit right now, I don't feel like I can handle a big confrontation. I don't know. It's getting so I don't want her around, which I hate, because I love her. I just need her to stop busying herself with my feelings. Maybe then she can start to deal with her own.

I was sitting in the living room tonight, thumbing through the piles of photos that I never take the time to put into albums, caressing with the tips of my fingers each image I had managed to capture of your father, when the phone rang. It was my mother, calling from her hotel room in Sydney. "Twenty-one weeks," I told her when she asked how far along in the pregnancy I was. "Disappointed?"

I didn't hear anything and thought perhaps we had been disconnected. Then her voice rang falsely bright in my ear. "Of course not, Sarah. What an awful thing to say to your mother. I'm happy for you. A baby will be a wonderful distraction."

I sighed. "Distraction from what, Mother? I should be distracted from losing my husband? You want me to just pretend Gavin didn't even exist, like there is anything in this world that could distract me enough to be able to pretend that? Jesus Christ, it hasn't even been three months!"

"Don't swear, dear," my mother said. "It's unattractive." Jesus Christ Jesus Christ Jesus Christ! I thought, then said, "And whom would I be trying to attract? A rich husband, perhaps? Someone who would be able to take care of me?"

"Now you're just being rude," she said quietly. I snorted. "Oh, I see. It's okay for you to be rude and say whatever's on your mind, but I'm supposed to be polite. *And* attractive. I get it." Neither of us said anything but didn't hang up. We just sat there silently, running up her international long-distance charges. I flipped through the stack of photos on my lap while I waited for her response, coming across an aged brown and crinkled shot of Nana Cecille. It's the only picture I have of her, in a moment that caught her off guard; she wasn't really looking at the camera but off into some faraway place beyond the photographer's shoulder. Her crinkled, round face was resting in her cupped hand, and a small secret smile danced on her lips as well as behind her warm hazel eyes. I'd venture to guess that she was thinking of Grandpa, for her expression is what I imagine mine to be when thoughts of your daddy fill my head.

"Hey, Mom," I said, cradling the photo carefully in my hand. "I just realized I only have one picture of Nana Cecille. Do you have any more you could send me?"

"No, not anymore. All that stuff was thrown out." I was dumbfounded. "*Thrown out?* You threw out all of her photo albums, the ones she kept her entire life? The ones with all the pictures of you growing up?"

She went on to try to justify her decision, telling me there was nothing worth remembering about how she grew up. "And besides," she said, "I gave you that one photo. Not to mention that awful chowder recipe and the little bottle she left for you. Remember?"

Of course I remembered. What I don't remember is the last time I saw Nana. Two years after my parents divorced and I no longer stayed with her, she died from massive heart failure. Your grandma didn't let me go to the funeral. She said at eight I was too young to understand what had happened, and, in a way, she was right. A small part of my child-mind kept my nana in front of her stove, endlessly stirring her chowder. Back then, I could maintain the illusion—most of my mind at that time in my life dripped with fantasy anyway—and my nana still being alive was just another belief I nursed. I sometimes imagined her on a long trip, searching to the ends of the earth for the fairies so she could thank them for their mystical dust.

My mother didn't give me the bottle and the chowder recipe until a year after the funeral, when she and David finally got around to having Nana's house cleaned out. The items—except the picture, which was added by your grandmother—were in a small box at the back of Nana's closet marked: FOR SARAH. What do you think was in that bottle? Fairy dust? I wish that it were. My tongue shattered the dream, erased the beauty of Nana's gift to me. Salt. That's all it was. I sat down hard in the middle of my bedroom and cried for hours. I think it was only then that I truly understood she was never coming back.

"Mom," I said, "I gotta go. I don't really feel like talking anymore." She was obviously relieved. "Okay, dear," she said. "You know where I am if you need anything."

"Yeah. You'll be the first person I call." I hoped

sarcasm traveled hard and fast over the phone lines. I hung up, tears standing like sharp needles in my eyes. I wondered what it will take for me to realize that your father is never coming back. What strange happening will convince me. As I said, I'm trying diligently to nurse the fantasy of his return, but it is getting harder and harder to do so. I keep trying to need him enough for him to come back. Maybe I should go talk to that therapist. How do you feel about my sharing our life with a stranger, someone who doesn't know us or your daddy?

I'm getting desperate. Time is passing quickly. Dr. Foster says that your fingers and toes are almost fully formed and that you are starting to swallow. How warm and comforting it must be inside my womb, drifting about in a silent ocean of peace. I wish that I could join you. I want to be ready when you come, ready to lavish myself upon you. Believe me, I want to do better by you than my mother did for me. Be patient with me, I swear I will come through.

Today was the hearing for the bastard who killed your father. I felt this was something I couldn't handle alone, so I asked Calista to come. I sat there in the courtroom next to her and began crying the moment they brought him in. It was the first time I'd ever seen him. He was young, not past thirty, and very handsome. Dark hair and bright eyes; I shuddered to think how much this killer actually resembles your father. He looks like someone your father might have even been friends with. Like someone he would have played basketball with at the park on Saturday mornings. I had pictured a creature swollen with alcoholism and age, ragged and hopeless. Instead, I saw a clean-cut young man who made a disastrous decision to get blind, stinking drunk with his buddies and drive himself home from a New Year's Eve bash. But I have no sympathy for him. He should have known better. His friends should have known better. If your father had been there, he would not have let this guy get behind the wheel. He would have taken and hidden this man's keys.

He pled guilty to vehicular manslaughter and was sentenced to eighteen months' jail time with the possibility of parole after seven. Plus five years of mandatory counseling for his drinking. He cried, begged for forgiveness. He claimed he was an alcoholic, that he needed only help, not prison. If you ask me, he needs a car to ram into someone he loves, then I might feel some pity for him. The judge felt the same way—she lectured him sternly on the responsibility he has to change the course of his life. I refused to make a victim impact statement; although I did say that it was your daddy who was this man's victim and there was no way for him to speak, now, was there? I saw a tearful shine surface in the judge's eyes when these words left my mouth, and somehow I just knew that along the way in this life, she too had lost a husband.

After his sentence was handed down, this man turned to me, tears running down his face, and said, "I'm so sorry. If there was any way I could take this back, I would. Please, please, know how sorry I am." I felt like throwing up. I was trembling as I stood to face him, and Calista grabbed my arm; I guess she thought I might hit him. But I didn't want to touch him. I saw the guilt swimming in his eyes and I told him that I hoped he burned in hell for taking your daddy away from us. Which was saying a lot since I don't really believe in hell. It's just the only thing I can imagine that is bad enough for him to endure besides someone impaling his wife with a car door and taking her life away and really, no matter what I say, I couldn't wish that on anyone.

It's a good thing he was well insured—it seems like he knew he might get himself into trouble someday because his insurance company called this afternoon and offered us an outrageously hefty settlement. Calista took the call, then conferred with me. I accepted their offer. No amount of money will ever, ever, ever make up for what happened to your father, but at least now we don't have to worry so much about getting by for the next couple of years. I can work at home, starting a few months after you are born, and we will be fine for quite a while.

When I said this to Calista, she disagreed. "I've been thinking you should maybe try and get back to work before the baby comes. Actually, I was going to clean your office this week, so you can start making some phone calls."

"I don't want to make any calls—I'm not ready to go back to work yet. And with this money coming, I don't have to."

She frowned. "Well, what about the therapeutic value? Getting back into the swing of things? You can talk to your clients, find out what's going on with them—"

"Didn't you hear me?" I said, interrupting her in my sharpest tone. "I'm not fucking ready. Or is that not all right with you?"

"Yeah, yeah, it's fine, Sarah." She shook her head. "God, sorry. I'm just trying to help."

"Well, quit it."

"I don't know how," she said, her words barely above a whisper. "Don't you know that about me by now?"

I felt you flutter today. An alien within me. Quickening, Dr. Foster called it. How strange, how exciting, how totally overwhelming. It just about knocked me right out of my chair. I was sitting at the kitchen table, wrapped around my own misery, choking down shredded wheat soaked in water because I haven't been to the store for milk, when I felt you. It felt like butterfly wings in my belly. At first I wasn't sure if it happened at all. It was quick, like the tug on a fishing line. Like bubbles traveling and popping their way through me. I thought I might just have gas. But then it was there again, this yank, this ripple along the edge of my womb. Did you kick me? Are you trying to remind me you are still here, that you are coming into this world soon so I'd better get my shit together?

The strangest thing of all is that this happened on your daddy's birthday. He would have been twenty-nine years old today. Last night I actually made him a cake. His favorite: chocolate with coconut-cream filling. I lit thirty candles—one extra for good measure

—sang "Happy Birthday," then ate the entire thing. That's where the remainder of the milk went.

I wonder how your daddy and I would have celebrated your movement? I can't think of a better birthday surprise. Would he have pressed his ear hard against you and demand that you do it again so that he could feel it? How much he wanted to be a part of your development. He wanted to teach you everything; he read to you about motorcycles and mechanics—do you remember? Or have you already forgotten the sound of his voice, the way he would press his mouth against the bare flesh of my belly and whisper to you through the marrow in my bones? His voice is still on our answering machine. I took the tape and put it in the living room stereo so that we can listen to him until we fall asleep. "Hi! Sarah and Gavin can't make it to the phone right now, but since you took the time to call, don't hang up—please leave us a message or we will hunt you down like the dog you are. See ya!" Do you already miss the sound of his voice?

After you wiggled a few more times, I went out to your daddy's tree to tell him what had happened. He did not appear, but in the bright clarity of the midday sun there was a fat-bellied robin perched on the branch above me. It twittered and chattered about something, seeming almost to respond to my words, as if it were trying to hold a conversation with me. Do you want to know something odd? That robin had green eyes—twin winking emeralds rimmed in tiny white feathers. I've never seen such a thing in all my life. Maybe I just imagined it. I don't know. Maybe I needed to see your daddy's eyes so deeply that they

appeared in whatever creature came closest to me.
God. That sounds so crazy.

I'm thinking more and more about you and me
going to see a therapist. I think it might be a good
idea. After this bird incident, maybe we had better
give it a try, huh? Maybe this person can help us.

When I pulled into the driveway tonight after my first counseling session, that blond woman next door waved and smiled at me from her porch. She was sitting huddled under a red-striped golf umbrella on her front steps, sipping from a mug of some steaming liquid. Her teeth were too white; they practically glowed in the dark. Bleached, probably. She's probably a bitch. She's just too pretty. Anyway, what kind of person sits outside in the middle of a rainstorm? I averted my eyes, pretending I hadn't seen her greeting, and hurried into the house.

So, I wonder what you think of Kate? She wasn't at all what I expected a therapist to be. She's young—early thirties, I think—which is kind of strange. I had thought she would need to be old, wizened somehow, dragged around the block a few times. Then she could say that she's been there. She's never even been married. She is beautiful: long, black, smooth hair, smoky chocolate eyes, and skin so porcelain, I immediately wanted to ask the name of the soap she uses. She's kind of heavy; I thought at first she might be pregnant too, but I didn't ask. Your father did that once when we ran into some woman he knew from high school. "When are you due?" he asked, all innocent and ready to congratulate. The woman's face turned to stone and she just walked away. "I don't think she's pregnant, Gav," I said. He smacked an open palm to his forehead. "Shit!" he said, and ran right after her, apologizing like nobody's business. Told her he left his glasses at home. His mistake entirely. Your father was like that. He hated to hurt people. He strove to make people feel special. When he found out it was his regular hairdresser's birthday, he went and bought her a card and some flowers and brought them back to her after his appointment. He was so sweet. It made me love him so much. Though it made me crazy sometimes too. Some women got the wrong idea when he'd do something nice, like help them get their car started on the side of a road. One of those damsels in distress even followed him back to our house. Boy, was she surprised to see me there! He never thought he might be sending out single-man, available vibes, he just believed in doing the right thing. . . .

What was I talking about? Right—Kate. She listened really well. I couldn't shut up. I told her about you, how we talk to each other—well, how you listen to me ramble. I told her about these letters to you, and she said they were probably the best thing I could possibly do for myself. I was glad when she said that. I was sort of afraid I've been doing something crazy, this writing to you, but Kate said that writing thoughts, memories, feelings, is extremely cathartic. She didn't ask a bunch of stupid questions, she just paused in the right places, and asked for details when I got quiet. She didn't say "Yes, but how does that make you *feel*?" We talked mostly about you. I know she knows from Dr. Foster that your daddy is gone, but I didn't bring it up. Maybe I'm testing her, I don't know. So far, though, I like her. We're going back day after tomorrow, since I found out that your daddy's health insurance covers us for another six months. Try to let me know if it's not okay with you. Kick my bladder or something. I'll be paying attention.

The goddamn water pipe under the house broke today. Your father was supposed to have patched the leak last summer, which he told me he did, but he must have been lying or maybe he did only a half-assed job. He was probably planning to take care of it, and now he's dead and he can't and I'm stuck mopping gallons of water off the fucking floor. He never did what he said he was going to do when he said he was going to do it. I had to ride him and ride him to get anything done around the house, then he'd bitch at me for being a nag. I hated that. He wanted to do things in his own sweet time, whenever it was convenient for him. It probably never even crossed his mind that I'd end up being the one who had to take care of all this shit.

When I woke up this morning and stepped onto the swampy carpet next to my bed, I screamed at your daddy. I swore at him. I threw things around the room. I'm fucking pissed that he's gone and I have to do all this. I knew I had to call a plumber and I didn't know what plumber to call because Gavin's the one who knew all the household maintenance crap. The reputable people in this town. The contractors that won't rip you off. I didn't know what to do. I cried. I called Calista and she had Mike come over and find the water turnoff for the house to at least stop any more flooding. Then he called a friend of his to come fix it and sat with me for a while before he began to help me mop up the mess. I hate that I was so helpless, so completely at a loss as to how to handle this crisis. I'm a grown woman, for Christ's sake, and I went hysterical when a pipe broke.

Dammit, Gavin should be here for this. He should be here like he said he was going to be here. To be your father, to fix the pipes, to hold me in the night and feel you kick against his hand. Oh, how I want someone to hold me. Calista is still here almost every day—even when I don't want her to be—putting her arms around me, but it is not the same. There is something inexplicable about the feeling of safety, of completion, like the fitting in of the last piece of a puzzle, when your husband's arms surround you. I think I miss that more than anything. More than sex. I can't imagine ever wanting sex again.

I wish so much there were someone I could talk to who understands all this. Dr. Foster was right, Kate has been helpful, she listens to me, but she has not been in this place. She has not run out of the house and around the street corner dressed only in her bathrobe because she thinks she has seen her dead husband in the crosswalk. She has not set two places on the dinner table every night, then remembered her husband is dead and won't ever be coming home for dinner again. She has not cried from some primal place within her, longing for the impossible to happen, for her husband to bring himself back to life. She can be my therapist and listen with all her heart, but she cannot know what this is, what my life has become.

I'm realizing more and more that Calista can't know either. What has risen between us feels vaguely like the distance you'll experience someday when you have gotten your period or lost your virginity and your best friend hasn't. Only the space that has separated Calista and me is wider and deeper. Uglier. At least you'll know your friend will eventually catch up —she'll get her period or sleep with her boyfriend— and then she'll know what you are going through and there you two will be, close as ever before. With my losing Gavin, the only way Calista could ever "catch up" with how I feel is if she loses Mike, and that is the very last thing I'd ever want to happen. I'm afraid the closeness we used to share—the unspeakable relief of having her listen to the craziness I feel and say, "yes, yes, I know exactly what you mean"—is gone. It has been swallowed by this huge, nasty thing called grief.

I told Kate at our last session that I think perhaps the only people who come close to knowing how I feel are those who have lost a limb. I've heard about the phenomenon of phantom itch, the impulse to scratch at a body part that no longer exists. This is exactly how I feel; I am overwhelmed by the impulse to talk to, laugh with, to cook for and clean for, to make love to a man who is no longer here. He has been amputated from my life. And I'm so sure that I can feel him, just as amputees are positive that they can feel the maddening itch of their leg or arm or foot or finger. I'm positive that if I just turn around at the right time, the right millisecond, he will be standing there, back in his designated spot in this life, right next to me.

And in order to convince myself that he will not be walking in the door after work, I have to open the box that holds his ashes. Let me tell you something right now: A person's ashes don't look anything like you'd imagine them to. In movies when ashes are scattered, they appear to be a fine dust, the powdery remains of a person drifting lightly through the air. But what they really are is pummeled bone. Chunks of a body. Big, burnt-up pieces of bones mixed in with some fluffy gray, fleshy ashes. I can't bring myself to touch them. So instead, I take out his death certificate. That convinces me, every time, that he is gone. What exactly am I supposed to do with that particular document anyway? Am I supposed to hang it up next to our marriage certificate, over our bed? Maybe I should put both documents in our scrapbook, as bookends of our life together. As if the sum of our relationship could be captured and bound, only to be left on a shelf and forgotten.

Spring . . .

Today the sun was brilliant in the sky and I was in the backyard again, kneeling beneath the spotty pink popcorn blossoms of your daddy's tree, when that blond woman came over to the fence and said hello. She introduced herself as Julie Patterson and told me that she just moved to Seattle for a new job with a local interior design firm and was very excited about it. Loved the Queen Anne neighborhood and so on, but did I happen to know where she could get some really good Chinese? I did *not* want to talk to this person. She was all lit up and happy with hope, for this new beginning of a better part of her life. She had better furniture than me. Whiter teeth. I hated her shining yellow bob, skinny-ass body, and cheerful doe eyes. She tucked her sleek hair behind one ear and asked, "Need any help in the yard?" I guess she thought I was gardening, not contemplating how on earth I am ever going to be able to work your daddy's ashes into the soil. She innocently inquired when you were due to be born. I was rude. I shouldn't have been, but I was. Told her your daddy was dead and I just wanted to be left alone. Told her to mind her own fucking business. Then I stomped to the house and slammed the back door.

I immediately longed to go and apologize to this woman; I am not really that kind of person, am I? Can you tell the difference between who I was and what your daddy's death has turned me into? Even I don't know this angry monster who shouts at poor, unassuming neighbors and swears at Jehovah's Witnesses. I called Calista, but Davie is sick with the croup and she couldn't take the time to talk. I contemplated calling other friends, the ones who offered help right after the accident, but felt, perhaps a bit stubbornly, that they should be calling me.

How uncomfortable people are with grief. They call only to say they have to be going. They offer their sympathy, then never come to listen and hold me when I cry. Even Calista is getting wrapped back up in the tiny details of her own life. Part of me feels like "Good, she doesn't understand what I'm going through anyway," but then a darker spot inside me says "Hey now, she's my best friend . . . she's supposed to be here for me no matter what." I know that sounds petty. I'm *feeling* petty. I haven't even told her that I went to my last appointment with Dr. Foster and had another ultrasound done. At twenty-four weeks you are about nine inches long and weigh almost a full pound. And I was right. You are a girl. A sweet bundle of pink. Your daddy and I were going to wait until you were born and be surprised, but something made me want to know right away. There is so little I can be certain of right now, your gender is at least something I can know for sure.

When I found out, I smiled up to the ceiling and said, "See, Gavin? What did I tell you?" I think the nurse thought I was loopy, but Dr. Foster just smiled right along with me; I had told her about my hunch. Now I can start thinking about what to name you. It's so important to give you a good name, a strong-sounding name, a name that your father would have loved to have roll off his tongue. I wish he would appear to me again and at least give me some suggestions. Neither of us really liked the idea of naming our children after family members, though I'd like to maybe name you Cecille, after my nana. I sort of believe a name should be entirely your own, given to you to match the uniqueness of your being.

I don't know. I'm rambling. I can't stop rambling. I start on one subject and end up thousands of miles from my point. If I even have one in the first place.

I hate how my mind works these days, drifting about in a sea of senselessness. I attempted to listen to my voice mail the other day, and for the life of me, I could not focus on the recordings. My clients are calling to see when I'm coming back—can I do the press releases for their Detroit dates in August? August. I can barely think about making it through tomorrow. As the messages played in my ear, my thoughts wandered to the day I married your father almost six years ago.

The sun rose full and glowing in the August sky, and we awoke in each other's arms. He said it didn't matter that the sun was shining because our smiles could have lit up the entire West Coast. He spent the morning with Mike, while Calista and I worked on making me beautiful. My dress—oh, my dress. I hope you will want to wear it on your wedding day. It is the simplest cut cream silk, long, straight sleeves, and a low-dipped cleavage line. Tiny fabric-covered buttons go up from the base of my spine to my neck. Calista swore like a banshee as she struggled to button me all up. No train, no lace, no pearls—simple. I didn't wear any shoes; I thought being a barefoot bride was somehow charming. Don't ask me where I get these ideas, I just get them.

We held the wedding service on the balcony of an old Victorian bed-and-breakfast, looking out over the sapphire shimmers of Elliott Bay. I descended a curving staircase, Calista leading the way in a sage summer dress, and you already know how your father said he felt when he saw me. What I didn't tell you about is the tear that slipped down his cheek when I joined him in front of the justice of the peace. We grinned at each other like idiots.

It was a small ceremony, only twenty people attended. Your grandmother, of course, was in Ethiopia or Thailand or some other godforsaken place without toilets, so she and David were unable to make it. Which was fine with both your father and me since we believed our decision to spend our lives together was a sacred happening and wanted to share it only with those closest to us. We thought that inviting your sixth cousin twice removed only to have him buy you a gravy boat was simply a ridiculous notion. Oh, what a day it was. What a brilliant, wonderful day. I didn't have a doubt in my mind that I had made the right decision.

Anyway, by the time I finished remembering all this, the messages had ended and I was weeping on the floor. Calista had come over to our house and used her key to let herself in because I had left the phone off the hook, I was so distracted by memories and my tears. When she kept getting a busy signal, she thought something awful might have happened. She thought I might have done something to us.

I feel like an utter fool, how I am still howling into my pillow, wrenched by even the thought of your father. I keep getting this somber image of Jackie Kennedy in my mind, how she held her head high, her spine erect, her chin lifted after JFK was killed. How strong she was. How utterly composed. At our last session, Kate said what I think are my crazy behaviors are perfectly natural, that the sudden death of a partner, especially early in a marriage, is one of the most devastatingly difficult losses a person can experience. She says there are stages of grief, and I will move through them according to my own needs. She says if I need to howl into a pillow, then I should. If I need to roll around in your daddy's clothes, then I should. I'm so glad she is there, telling me I am sane.

But what I really need her to tell me is this: What can I do to keep the grief from you when I have to go through it? Right now it feels as if it will go on forever. I am yelling at neighbors. I am angry at Calista for having a husband and a beautiful little boy, for pushing me to get on with my life, for not having a clue about what I'm going through. I am staring at myself naked in the mirror, trying to remember my body before you took me over. There is this weird shadowy line going down from my belly button. Dr. Foster says it's completely normal, but I keep looking at it like some foreign invader took a pen and marked my skin. I look at my enormous body—up fifty-four pounds now, goddammit—and try to draw your daddy next to me in the mirror, try to pull him back from wherever he's gone. He can't hear me calling for him anymore, I guess. Or maybe I am starting to not need him so much.

I still get such overwhelming feelings of his presence, especially as I hold his ashes beneath his tree, as if he were urging me on, *yes, Sarah, yes—this is where you should put me . . . this is where I am and where I'll stay.* I can almost hear his voice in my head. I haven't told Calista or Kate about this. Only you. I still can't bury him. Not yet.

I wish there were a way for me to comfort you, to hold you already and whisper reassurances in your perfect little ears. Maybe if I can reassure you, I can reassure myself. I want so much to see you, to memorize your precious face; I feel you so often now, pressing against my womb, tossing and turning in the night. Am I keeping you awake? I try to lie still on the couch, but I am starting to get too wide to fit comfortably on the cushions. The muscles in my lower back have melded into a tight iron band. I may have to return to the bed, and I'm not sure if I can do it. There's so much I'm not sure of. Are you scared that I am supposed to be your mother? I know I am.

I wish Gavin were here. He was so good at helping me put life into perspective. He focused the kaleidoscope of my confusion into reality, so that I could see what was happening through clearer eyes. I feel blind, like I'm frantically reaching out for a steady arm to guide me, and the person who is connected to that arm has walked away and left me alone, stranded on a busy downtown street corner.

I was in the kitchen this morning, eating an ever so healthy breakfast of cinnamon toast and Milk Duds, when there was a knock at the door. But when I answered it, there was only a white wicker basket sitting on the porch. It overflowed with fruit and little gold boxes, along with a note that said "I am so sorry for your loss. If you ever feel like talking, I am right next door."

I assumed our new neighbor did this. Miss Perfect Long-legged, Perky-tits Julie Patterson. Who the hell does she think she is? I thought as I slammed the basket onto the coffee table and flopped myself down on the couch. This woman doesn't know me. What kind of person gives a stupid fruit basket to a stranger? Still, I was the tiniest bit curious, so I reached for one of the boxes for a peek. Inside were chocolates: dark and rich, their surfaces smooth and shiny, perfectly tempered. Placing a small square on my tongue, I had to close my eyes from the pleasure. Julie Patterson didn't mess around. I was suddenly embarrassed for eating

Milk Duds, and then annoyed I had been so easily pulled in by her cheap attempt to play nice. She must really need me to like her, I thought. Snatching the basket off the table, I strode across the lawn and pounded on her screen door.

"Thanks, but no thanks," I said, holding out the basket to her. She looked confused. "Nice thought," I continued, "but I really don't need your pity." I set the basket on the porch and spun around to leave. Julie called out to me. "Wait, please. I didn't mean to offend you. You've misunderstood. Can I make you a cup of tea or something? Please . . . ?"

I don't really know what it was that made me stop. Something in her voice maybe. I almost felt like I had heard it before. I told her I would come in just for a minute, privately thinking I would simply check out her house and see what other furniture I could hate her for having. It was just as I thought: two plump, French-floral sofas, mahogany tables, and billowy, silken drapes graced the living room as though she had lived there for years, carefully choosing each piece to complement the others. Part of me wanted to punch her perfectly chiseled face.

Leading me toward the back of the house, she asked me to excuse the piles of fabric and drawings that were spread out over the dining room. "Big Mercer Island house I'm doing. Thirty-five hundred square feet. It's a nightmare." I nodded—like I knew what she meant. Pushing through swinging shuttered doors, she motioned for me to sit at her slate-blue kitchen table. "Is peppermint tea okay for you . . . ?" she asked, trailing off. She grinned, tilted her head. Those damn white teeth again. "I'm sorry, I don't know your name."

"Sarah," I told her, keeping my voice closed. I watched as she poured the tea into large, obviously hand-painted mugs. I figured Miss Interior Decorator probably did them herself. She added two sugars to mine, as if she knew I always take just that amount, without even asking me. It was a little spooky. I looked around her kitchen: It practically sparkled. The sun wiggled through the windows and bounced rainbow prisms off the checkerboard floor. The blinding white Formica counter was neatly topped with a toaster, a blender, and a bread basket; the uncluttered space was also spotless. Even the ceramic bowl on the table in front of us, filled with a healthy pile of apples and oranges, was dust free. I could not remember my kitchen ever being this clean. I asked how she kept it this way. A tiny melancholy smile eased to her lips, and then she said, "When you're alone, you fill the time with whatever busies you." She stretched her arm out, gesturing across the room. "What you see here, Sarah, is the product of a woman with a lot of time on her hands."

She asked how long I had been a widow. It was the first time someone spoke that ugly title aloud. Not even Dr. Foster or Kate has used the term in reference to me. It was disarming, and felt slightly uncomfortable, as though I had accidentally slid my right foot into a left shoe. But despite this, I found myself telling her it had been just over three months since the accident and that you were due the end of June. That you were a girl, like I told your father you would be. Tears stood precariously in her eyes, and she grasped my

hands and said, "How lucky you are to have this miracle on the way. How wonderful to have a part of your
husband inside you, a part of him to be with you
forever." It had not really crossed my mind lately to
think of myself as lucky. But the fervent way she
spoke, with such longing in her expression, made me
glow for a moment. Glow with pure gratefulness for
your existence.

We sat in silence for a few minutes, sipping our
tea, and I was just about ready to stand up and leave,
when Julie finally spoke, her voice quiet and tender.
"I truly am sorry for your loss, Sarah. I know what
you're going through." My heartbeat became very
loud at those words, and I sat motionless, utterly mes-
merized, as she told me the story of three years ago in
Los Angeles, when her husband, James, had been the
victim of a drive-by shooting. He had been walking
down the street, heading to the corner market on a
break from the law office where he had just made
senior partner, when a car swung madly around the
corner and someone started shooting at him. A crack
dealer angry that James had successfully defended a
rival. "My Jimmy," she said, "he lived for three days
with a bullet lodged in his brain. He was unconscious
the entire time. I held his hand and swore to him that I
could not live without him, so he had better wake up.
I shook him, slapped his face, did everything I knew
how to make him hear me. But still, he just slipped
away, without ever waking up to say good-bye." Her
voice rattled as she spoke; I recognized the tremble.
"He made a good living representing bastards like the
boy who killed him. Drug dealers pay hefty retainers,
but all the money in the world didn't keep him alive."

After hearing this, I felt horrible for being such a bitch to her, for passing judgment without knowing a damn thing about who she was. I apologized profusely for my rude behavior, but she only flapped her hands in the air next to her ears and told me there was no need; that being a bitch is sometimes all a woman has to hold on to. Said Kathy Bates spoke those words in some Stephen King movie and Julie thought it was one of the most profound statements she had ever heard.

When I asked her if she still felt angry about losing Jimmy, she cackled, a sound the color of tar. "Of course," she said. "Of course I get angry. But eventually, you realize how much energy gets wasted on fueling that anger. You realize that it will get you nowhere. I came here to start again, to get away from everything that sucks that anger back up to the surface."

How strong she sounded. So grounded and determined to survive. We sat at that table for a long time. I was so relieved to have someone who might actually know what I've been feeling, I pretty much poured myself out to her. She listened to me intently, all about my fury with the man who killed your daddy, about my fear of being alone and raising you, about the mind-numbing loneliness that reaches inside me and makes me afraid I might not make it through another day. And the best thing was, she didn't say things happen for a reason, she didn't say do this do that and everything will be okay. She didn't say it was a matter of time. She just listened. She cupped her hands and gave me a place to put my feelings. Somehow, it was better than Kate, better than Calista, both so well meaning. But Julie, when Julie nodded at my words I knew she was truly understanding what I was saying. There is something precious in that understanding. Something strong that is beginning to seep into me. Do you feel it?

It has been only a little over a week since Julie and I met, but it feels as though we have known each other forever. I've decided not to ask why or how these things happen—the synchronicity of my needing someone like Julie and her sudden appearance next door—since most often those answers are impossible to find. I am simply basking in the pleasure of this woman saying "yes, I know" and being sure she means it.

We've been spending the last several evenings either at her house or mine, simply talking, sharing the little details that form the foundation of a lasting connection. During our second or third conversation, I found out she is so thin because of a thyroid problem. "You call that a problem?" I asked jokingly. Of course, the grass is always greener; she confessed that she'd give just about anything to trade her perky chest in for a pair of full, round breasts like mine. At which point I smiled, showed her the dark red divots in my shoulders where my bra straps dig in deep, and told her she might want to think again.

Last night, warmed by fluffy blankets and good jazz, we burrowed into the cushions of her comfy sofa and looked through her wedding album. Jimmy didn't look much like I expected him to: He was shorter than Julie by about three inches, and wider than her by about ten. But Julie touched his face in the photos with a reverence I recognized as one known only to those who have felt true love, the type of love that does not need to be explained. "He was my soul mate," she said as fat tears rolled down and splashed on the pages of the album in her lap. "My very best friend. Still, it took us so many years to learn how to get things right . . . we were just getting past all the bullshit when he died. We were learning about compromise, we were talking about finally having a baby. Ten years just wasn't enough, you know?" I nodded, hoping my presence gave her comfort. Hoping I was giving her at least a portion of the empathy she was so generously sharing with me.

Then, this morning, she came over to make sure I was getting out of bed and had something planned for my day. "Even if it means the only thing you manage to do is take a shower and put on some lipstick," she said. "I promise, doing one small thing will make you feel like you climbed a mountain. Make your list short." When I looked at her doubtfully, she insisted, "Really, I mean it. Write it down. You'll find strength in being able to cross everything off."

I am so grateful for her, for all her strength and support, as well as how freely she has opened her own pain to me. The raw truth I've seen in her eyes proves to me again and again that she, too, has felt everything I am feeling, and this has made me more willing to take her advice. So, I accomplished three small tasks today: braiding my hair, making the bed, and hanging up my clothes instead of dressing from a messy pile on the floor. Amazingly, I find myself looking forward to more of those little victories; like I'm fighting a war against grief and might actually win a few battles.

Calista hasn't met Julie yet, although I've told her about my new neighbor. "Her husband died young too," I said. "She really gets what I've been going through." Calista didn't want to hear another word about it. "I can't believe you'd make friends so quickly with a complete stranger," she said. "You never have before." I paused before I answered, tried to keep the sarcasm from my voice, but failed. "Well, I've never had a dead husband before either." She hasn't called me since.

After that conversation I spoke a little to Julie about the situation, about the problems I was having with Calista's pushing me to move on. Julie tilted her head and looked sincerely sorry I was going through a tough time with my best friend, but the only thing she'd say was "Sounds like you two really need to work some things out. Definitely not my place to butt in." Her rational nature is slightly annoying.

I don't know what to do. It's getting so I'd rather spend time with Julie than Calista. I feel like such a child for not being able to just talk to Calista about the frustration I've felt toward her since your daddy passed away. I just know it'll be the kind of conversation that after it's over will make me feel like someone took a crowbar to my insides. I don't know if I can handle Calista's screwed-up emotions right now—I'm having enough trouble juggling my own.

After I got home from my twenty-sixth-week checkup with Dr. Foster this morning, your Auntie Calista appeared at our back door, unannounced. It was the first time we had seen each other since Julie and I began spending so much time together. She was surprised to find me showered and dressed, furiously cleaning the kitchen. When I said I was accomplishing so much at Julie's suggestion, protectiveness hung like a dark flag over her face. I could tell how pissed off she was that some other person had been able to motivate me. "Who is this woman anyway?" she demanded. "I mean, what do you know about her?"

I threw the sponge into the sink, slopping water up onto the counter. Spinning around to face her, I let my anger loose. I didn't plan it—it just happened. She tapped a vein and the words simply bled out of me. "Goddammit, Calista, who the hell do you think you are, my mother? I fucking don't need you to tell me who I can and can't be friends with, okay? Julie understands me. She's been where I am. You haven't. I'm so tired of your pretending to know what I need. You don't. I'm not like you . . . I can't just put on a happy face and act like my life is everything I want it to be. My husband is *dead,* Calista. *DEAD!* Do you even get that? Do you get that I am alone and about to bring my dead husband's child into this world? Do you have any idea how fucking overwhelmed I am by that? And here's you, pushing me to just move on and smile and laugh and go back to work because it's easier for you if I do. God forbid the way I deal with my grief should *inconvenience* you."

Calista slowly backed up to the refrigerator as I spoke. She pressed her hand hard over her mouth and shook her head. Her eyes were widened and filled with tears, and I wanted to stop, but I couldn't. Months of holding in my feelings caught up to me at that moment. The words just kept tumbling out. "I am so *sick* of the way you gloss over everything shitty in your life. You need to deal with your pain, Calista. That's why you can't deal with mine . . . you don't know how to deal with your own. You tell yourself you do . . . you push it down and call that dealing with it. You've done that ever since I've known you. Well, let me tell you something, sister, all that shit is going to come up and bite you in the ass. One of these days you're gonna fucking explode." Seeing the look on her face brought tears to my own eyes, and I tried to soften my tone. "Calista, listen. Can't you please understand that I'm just trying to deal with all this pain? I'm trying to get it out so it doesn't suffocate me. So it doesn't suffocate my baby. Talking with Julie helps me do that. Please, I need you to understand that. I need you too, just in a different way. Isn't that okay? Can't I get different things from different people?"

I could have taken a bite out of the silence that filled the air between us. Calista stared hard at me, her eyes narrowing, the tears still slipping down both our faces. I slowly sunk to the floor, my legs splayed out in front of me, my hard belly resting on my thighs. I held out my hands, palms-up, as if to say "What? Tell me what I need to say to get through to you."

Calista's voice was very quiet when she finally began to speak. It was almost a whisper. "You don't think I understand? You don't think I've been patient? Jesus Christ, you're selfish, Sarah. Your grief *has* been an inconvenience. I know you're in pain. I know you are. You don't think I can see it? It drips out of you. The room fills with your pain everyplace you go. And I'm sorry if you think I've been pushing you. I never meant to. I've never dealt with grief like this, okay? I don't know what I've been doing any more than you have. So don't you stand there and tell me how I'm dealing with it is wrong. I'm dealing with it the only way I know how, just like you. And I've been here every fucking day, Sarah, whether or not I wanted to be. Did you ever bother to fucking ask me if I *wanted* to be here?" Her voice grew increasingly shrill with every sentence; her hands pressed into white-knuckled fists next to her hips. "Have you once asked how Mike is dealing with losing his best friend? *Have you?* On top of all your pain, I've been taking care of his too. I don't fucking have time to deal with my own. So I'm glad Julie's here for you. I'm glad that in only two weeks she has been able to give you everything I haven't been able to, so now I can go home and stop worrying about you. Maybe now I can get some sleep." She smacked herself on the forehead with the heel of her palm. "Oh, wait, I forgot. I have a two-year-old . . . I don't get to sleep." And then she laughed, incredulous. "You know what I just realized, Sarah? You've turned into your worst nightmare: a selfish, mindless bitch. You've turned into your mother." Before I could respond, she was out the back door.

I tried to go after her, but getting up from the floor with the weight of you pulling me off balance took too long, and by the time I got to the front lawn, she had already driven off. I wanted to call her tonight, but thought we both could use some time to calm down. I feel horrible for going off on her like that . . . especially since a few of her words hit home. What *was* I doing, telling her how to deal with her feelings, when I've been so angry with her for telling me how to deal with mine? I have been acting like my mother—completely dismissive of everyone's needs but my own. I need to apologize. I need to thank her for everything she's done. I need to make everything okay between us. I need my best friend.

Calista didn't return my calls for three days. Of course, as luck would have it, when she finally did call me back last night, Julie happened to be over. She had been telling me about the first month after Jimmy died, when she couldn't go to work or even leave her house. "Who's there?" Calista asked when she heard Julie's voice. I sighed and told her—reluctantly. There was fury in every breath of Calista's response. "Huh. Well. Guess I'll talk to you tomorrow." She hung up, and I began to feel awful all over again, as well as panicked that I was making the wrong choice in spending any time with Julie when Calista has been there for me practically my entire life.

Julie looked concerned as I set the phone down. My hand was shaking. "Everything okay?" she asked.

I shrugged. "Yeah. Well . . . actually, no. Calista and I had a blowout the other day. A pretty major one. She's ticked about how much I've been hanging out with you."

"Hmmm . . ." Julie mused. "So, what did you say to her?"

"I told her to mind her own business, basically, plus a whole lot of other stuff about her own inability to deal with her feelings . . . old stuff. Stuff that's really not my place to give her shit about, you know? But now I'm thinking maybe she was right on a few things."

"Really. Like what?"

"Well, like maybe I should be spending more time with her. She *is* my best friend. She's been there for me a long time—maybe I'm not giving her enough of a chance to understand what all this is like for me." I swallowed, trying to work up the courage to speak what was brewing in my mind.

Julie leaned toward me on the couch and looked intent. "What exactly are you saying, Sarah?"

"I'm saying . . . well, maybe I'm saying we *shouldn't* be spending so much time together. I mean, we barely know each other."

She sighed. "Are you telling me you don't want to be friends anymore because it's doing damage to your relationship with Calista? Or does part of it have to do with the fact that you're scared because spending time with me is making you feel better and you're not sure if you *want* to feel better? Feeling better makes you feel guilty, right?"

I pulled my chin into my chest and raised one eyebrow at her. "*Excuse* me?"

"It's okay," she said gently. "I know how you're feeling. But look, just because you push me away doesn't mean I'm going anywhere. It doesn't work that way. I'm sorry things are tough with Calista right now, but you have to understand . . . when I came here, when I looked at my house, I was totally over-whelmed by this feeling of 'yes, here, you need to be here.' I trusted that feeling even though I didn't know why I had it. Now I know why. I needed to meet you. You needed to meet me. That's just the way it is, okay?" I knew what she meant—synchronicity. She quieted her voice even further. "Listen, Sarah. The people who helped me after Jimmy died—really, truly helped me—were the ones that were just *there*, you know? They didn't ask what I needed, they just gave it to me. They were a constant presence in my life. So here I am, girlfriend, being present, whether you like it or not." She slapped her hands on the thighs of her jeans and moved to leave. I didn't know what to say except "Okay." I simply didn't have the strength to go on with the conversation. I felt depleted by all this confrontation; first Calista, then Julie. I also felt a little blindsided by how both of them called me on a couple of things I haven't wanted to think about. These are wise women—I respect them—I figured I should take their thoughts to heart.

So, this morning, I sat beneath the cherry tree and forced myself to consider what my two friends had said. Calista was right. I have been incredibly selfish; I've never once acknowledged all she's done for me over the last few months; never said "thank you." I've been too busy being annoyed with her. Then suddenly I'm telling her about how wonderful Julie is for me. No wonder she got pissed. Julie was right too—feeling better does scare me. Part of me is feeling like I'm doing some kind of dishonor to your daddy by not being so paralyzed by my pain anymore, by wanting to take a small step forward with this new person in my life. I guess on some level I wanted to push Julie away for the relief she's brought me.

I also thought about how strangely comforted I am by the tenderness in Julie's voice, how even though I've known her only a few weeks, I couldn't imagine not hearing that voice every day. I almost crave it. It suddenly struck me *why* I turned around and went into her house the day I returned the fruit basket: She sounds eerily like my Nana Cecille. That low, rumbling warmth in every word. It might sound crazy, but I'm thinking maybe Nana's spirit is reaching out to me through Julie. Maybe Nana knows how much I need her right now. Maybe Julie's appearance is Nana's way of telling me she's still here.

A little while ago Julie brought over a pot of spaghetti but didn't stay to eat with me. When I tried to apologize for what I had said last night, how I tried to push her away, she made a "pffft" sound with her lips. "No big deal. So. I'll leave you alone tonight." She wagged a playful finger at me. "But I'll be here in the morning, honey. You can count on it."

What an incredible day. I was at my appointment with Kate, telling her about the drama going on between Julie, Calista, and me, when I was suddenly overwhelmed by such guilt. Guilt for how awful all this must be for you. Here I am, wrapped up in all these peripheral issues with Julie and Calista, slowly starting to feel like I'm not so much at the mercy of my pain, when maybe I'm just fooling myself. Maybe I'm simply distracting myself from grief, pushing it down, pressing it into you.

I told Kate how much I wish I could comfort you, and she said that I could. She said that visualization can be a powerful tool in healing and offered to lead me inside myself to meet you. At first I thought she was a little bit nuts to suggest such a thing. But then I thought if I can write all these letters to you, if I can already believe in the strength of your tiny spirit, why shouldn't I be able to reach down deep and find you with my mind?

So Kate lowered the blinds and turned off the

overhead light. She had me curl fetal (well, as fetal as possible considering the cumbersome bulge of you) on the lavender couch where I usually just sit. She sat back in her chair and then began with her lullaby voice to lead me through a long session of breathing and relaxation exercises, the same type of exercises I have been practicing for your birth. Soon my body was twisty and loose as a pile of rubber bands.

I closed my eyes and Kate asked me to picture the flow of blood through my veins, the sinewy ropes of muscle tissue along with the fatty deposits that I know must line my skin. I saw my heart pumping with aching determination, my lungs pulling in and pushing out behind my ribs. Redness and wet swirled around as I traveled through my stomach, where behind the shadows I thought I saw the crumbled remains of my lunch, spinach salad and a blueberry muffin.

And then, finally, to my womb. To your dwelling place. I saw your tiny body, your head so much bigger than the rest of you right now, your thumb popping in and out of your mouth. You blinked in my direction. The walls pulsed around us, breathing and moving in concert with my lungs. You floated peacefully, the cord that connects us drifting about in a silent oceanic rhythm. I did not speak, but felt that you could hear me. I told you how much I adore you. I promised with everything in me to take care of you, to protect you and give you everything you will ever need in this world. That no matter the chaos that still churns inside me, we will be all right. I promised you that I will share everything about your daddy with you, so it will be as if he is with us, if not in body, always in spirit. I felt your eyes connect with mine, and it was as though an invisible tether of understanding instantly wove it-self between us. No words were spoken, no tears were shed, but peace rushed over me like a waterfall, and for the first time since your daddy died, I felt my heart smile.

This visualization thing is a bit tricky. I can't really say for sure that I went inside myself or if I just imagined myself doing it. You could tell me. Did you see me there? Or maybe you just felt me. It wasn't like I could reach out and touch you; I couldn't hold your hand or caress your cheek. It was all very cerebral. A meeting of our minds. But I saw you. There was something felt between us, an understanding that we will make it through. For the past few months I have felt so horrible, so powerless, as you endured my emotional house of horrors, and now, somehow, I feel strongly that we will survive. Wait. Not only survive, but thrive. Finally, I am beginning to feel something that I did not think I would ever experience again. I am beginning to feel hope.

At yesterday's appointment Kate suggested I do my best to heal things with Calista. "Reach out to her," Kate said. "She's your best friend. You know how to work it out. You've already done the hard part: being honest with each other about your feelings. Now love each other anyway. You said that's what family does, right?"

So, swallowing my fear of another confrontation, I called Calista this morning and asked her to come over. "This baby girl inside me has put in a request for chocolate," I said, finally sharing this news with her. "Bring some, okay? We're probably going to need it." She laughed, but I heard a small sob at the back of her throat. "Oh, sweetie," she cried. "It's a girl? Tell her I'll be right there!" I smiled, in my heart knowing that our friendship would not crumble beneath the weight of the hard truths we had told; rather, it would grow.

Calista arrived and set a box of chocolate croissants on the kitchen counter. We looked at each other, lips trembling, and said in unison, "I'm sorry." Hugging long and hard, we cried, me more so than her. It's amazing how many tears one person can produce; I'd have thought I'd be all dried up by now.

We settled at the kitchen table. "I never should have said all those awful things," Calista said, sucking at the edge of a croissant, trying to get a hunk of chocolate out of the middle. I was already on my second pastry, and taking the last bite, I rubbed my belly in a circle of satisfaction. "Of course you should have," I responded. "I'm glad we both said what we said. We got a lot of stuff out into the open. And please know how sorry I am that I haven't been more grateful for everything you've done for me. . . ." I paused, fighting the tears that once again tightened the muscles in my chest. "I mean, everything you've done for *us*. I know I've been a major pain in the ass. I probably still will be." She smiled and took my hand in hers before I went on. "I thought a lot about what you said, and you were right—everyone has to deal with their feelings in their own way. So. Let's just agree to stop interfering with each other's shit. You have your shit and I have mine—let's just hold hands while we wade through our separate piles, okay?" She nodded, eyes shiny, and squeezed my fingers tight. I continued. "One more thing—I really want you to meet Julie. She's very cool. Plus, she is going to be in my life and I want you to know her." Calista looked hesitant, about ready to shake her head, so I held up my hand in warning. "Uh-uh-uh! Give her a chance. For me, okay? You don't have to be her best friend. We'll just have dinner or something. Chicks-night-in at my place." She finally relented, agreeing to keep an open mind. Before she left to pick Davie up from the sitter's, we made plans for this Friday, as long as Julie was available.

Then, after Julie got home from work tonight, she came over and made me put on my tennis shoes to go for a walk. She would not take no for an answer. "The baby," she said, "if anything, you need to do it for her. You barely have two months. Now, *come on!*" She leaned down and pressed her mouth against my belly. "You want some exercise, don't you, peaches?" she said. "Tell your mama to get her butt moving!" I couldn't believe it when she called you peaches, what Nana used to call me. Talk about spooky. Not evil-bad spooky, more like psychic-strange spooky.

She's right, of course. I do need to exercise. She sat me down and brushed my hair into a ponytail, then picked out a flouncy summer dress that just barely contains the cannonball of my belly. How lovely I looked: torn-up running shoes and a cotton dress. I promise to dress myself better when you arrive. I don't want to embarrass you.

The air was thick with the warm, misty purple hue of twilight. I spent the dark months of winter practically quarantined in the house, and now, suddenly, I have emerged into the eruption of spring. Bloodred rhododendrons and fragrant lilacs shouted at our every turn; happy rows of blossoming daffodils and tulips stood to attention as we passed them by. The Northwest is such a beautiful place to live. Seattle gets a bad rap for all the rain we supposedly endure, but what people don't understand is the stunning beauty that arises from the moisture more than makes us forget the days of umbrellas and galoshes. It makes us thankful for them. The sight of Mount Rainier after an afternoon storm, floating against a cotton-candy sky, will knock the air right out of you. It will make you grateful that you are alive to see it.

As we rounded the neighborhood, for the most part, Julie and I did not speak. It was difficult enough for me to convince one foot to propel itself in front of the other. Julie seemed to sense this, reaching now and again for my hand when I began slowing to a stop in the middle of the sidewalk, as if I were a wind-up toy whose key had run out of twist.

At times, things still seem so peripheral around me; when I turn to look at something, it jerks out of my line of sight. I can't always bring the world into focus. I know life is going on: Cars are being washed, people are going to work, houses are being built, other babies are being born, but it isn't always possible to reconcile myself to the reality of these happenings. It's the strangest sensation of disconnection, as if I'm existing on a slightly separate plane from the rest of the world.

I voiced this feeling to Julie, who simply nodded emphatically and said, "You are in a different world than everyone else. You're in the world of Trying to Heal. Don't worry, the feeling eventually goes away. Just be where you need to be, and I'll make sure you don't collide with anything destructive." I asked her about Friday night and she said it sounded like a wise idea. She promised to bring dessert.

I have to admit, it really did feel wonderful to move my body; I felt you squirm all around inside me, bouncing on top of my bladder. Are you going to be an athlete like your father? Am I going to have to endure lectures from you about how to keep in shape?

Great, that's just what I need. I guess it should make you happy, then, that Julie and I made a date for tomorrow night for another walk.

The dusky night air felt sweet in my lungs, saturating my senses, almost like a drug. And now I'm exhausted, so I'll cut this short. Let's go climb in bed. Maybe I can manage to read you a story before I pass out.

I spent most of today getting ready for the dinner with Calista and Julie, cooking the first true meal outside of the microwave I've made since your daddy died. (There it is again, that sharp pain in my gut as I write those words . . . I wonder if it will ever go away.)

The dinner went as well as I could have hoped. I served pasta with a Parmesan cream sauce, lemon-buttered asparagus, and crusty French bread. My plan was to fill any silence between the three of us with calories. I did the most talking while we ate, and my two friends quietly eyed each other; Calista asking safe questions like "Could you pass the butter, please, Julie?" Julie was a little more daring, inquiring about Davie's age and behaviors, and at which salon Calista had gotten such a fabulous haircut. I tried to keep the conversation going—I wanted so much for them to like each other.

After we finished eating and moved to the living room, Julie and Calista continued to stalk each other carefully, feeling out intentions and histories and humors. I hadn't gone into great detail with either of them about the personality of the other; with girl-friends you all either get along or you don't. As I lowered myself next to Calista on the couch, I could see her taking in Julie's graceful frame and I hoped she wouldn't take to hating Julie right off because of her annoying beauty, as I had. I ached to say "It's okay, Calista; it's not her fault she's so thin," but I knew it wouldn't make a difference. Calista would think what-ever she wanted.

We chatted for a while about Julie's new job and what she thought about Seattle, and thankfully the tension finally broke when Julie leaned forward in her chair and asked, "Do either of you happen to know where a woman can get a vibrator in this town? Mine broke." I thought Calista might burst right open laughing. Julie smiled but remained serious. "No, really, I mean it. In L.A. there are sex shops on every freaking corner, but here I haven't seen a one. Is there, like, a designated smut neighborhood or something? Can somebody give me a map?" It was as simple as that: The bond between the two materialized in that moment, with Calista offering to spend Saturday guid-ing Julie to all the respectable sex emporiums. How connections are forged between women is a mysteri-ous thing; a woman just knows, her gut immediately tells her when she has met an ally. For Calista, it was discovering her and Julie's mutual yen for sex toys. "You know why vibrators are better than men?" Julie asked. Calista, as if on cue, chimed in. "Yup . . . vibrators have five speeds." I was a little baffled by this instant rapport—I never would have guessed the tie that would bind them—but, at the same time, I was incredibly relieved it was there to be found.

Julie produced the box of Godiva chocolates she had brought for dessert, and for the rest of the evening we settled into the comfort that arises from knowing you are surrounded by kindred spirits. As we let a food coma ease over us, Julie told us about reentering the dating scene. "It took me two years before I could go on my first date after Jimmy died." She put two caramels in her mouth at once and moaned with pleasure as she swallowed them down. "God, I love chocolate. More convenient than sex and much less messy." Calista raised her peanut butter cup in salute. "Amen, sister!" Julie giggled and wiped her mouth with the back of her hand. "Anyway. It was a shitty night. All I could do is think about Jimmy, how he would have hated this idiot guy who asked me out. You'll know what I mean pretty soon, Sarah." I shook my head, the tears pricking the muscles in my throat. Calista reached out to hold my hand, and Julie started crying too, saying, "What an idiot I am. Me and my big stupid mouth. Sarah, I'm so sorry. What a shitty thing to say." I knew she didn't mean to cause me any pain, but I can't even begin to imagine being with another man right now.

The night ended a short while later when Mike called to see if Calista was ever coming home. After hugging us both, Julie staggered through the backyard to her house. Calista gathered her coat and purse, then reached to embrace me. "You didn't tell me she looked like a Barbie doll," she scolded playfully, her voice muffled into my neck. She pulled back and smiled. "It's a good thing the woman's so damn down-to-earth, or I might've had to hate her."

"Yeah, she's great. But she's not you . . . okay?"

"Stop it," Calista teased. "Or I'll have to kiss you."

After watching her drive off, I washed my face and slipped beneath the cool sheets, feeling peaceful. Once again we are alone. But somehow, tonight, I am not quite so lonely.

I was awake for two hours today before I remembered that your daddy is dead. I got showered, ate breakfast, and spent an hour in my office tackling the reorganizing chores of going back to work before it hit me. You gave my belly a violent kick and suddenly it was as if I were thrown smack up against a brick wall. I'm having his baby in two months, I thought. And Gavin is dead.

How strange that your daddy was not the first thing in my mind. The itch to work has been tickling the back of my brain for a few weeks now; I've been wondering how my clients are doing with the substitute publicist. I've felt stronger lately, especially since my visualization session with Kate, like I can actually think about the future and believe in my ability to take care of you. When I realized I had not thought of your daddy this morning, I experienced a guilt so completely overwhelming, I felt like I might throw up. As I sat on the linoleum in the bathroom, I thought that it is probably a good sign that I'm thinking of other things before Gavin. But still. It has been only four months. I suppose he would want me to try to move on. To begin to heal. To not wallow in the memory of him. I just miss him so much. I know it's stupid to say, but I wish he were here to tell me what to do.

So, of course, I went out to his tree and waited for him to come to me. I talked to him, I cried and asked him to show me that he was not hurt by my momentary forgetting. I listened to the squeals of pleasure sing out from neighborhood children playing in their blossoming yards, thankful that I could smile at the sound. The sun was hazy behind the stretched gauze of clouds, and a slightly chilly breeze stirred the air. When I stood up to go back into the house, there was the green-eyed robin perched noiselessly on a branch above me. Next to him sat another bird, a smaller robin with a paler, earthy-red chest. A female maybe. She held a small stack of twigs in her beak. I think they are making a home here. Perhaps that is your daddy's way of telling me he is going nowhere, he is staying where he belongs. Here, with us, whether I am thinking of him every minute of the day or not, he is still at home.

Calista brought Davie over to our house today so I could watch him while she got some errands done. When she called this morning and asked if I could do this for her, I was afraid it might be too much for me. I wasn't sure I could handle it, but now, afterward, I am so happy I agreed. I'm suddenly so excited for your arrival, the first true excitement I have felt since the beginning months of your life, the excitement I shared with your daddy. I feel the urge to go shopping for tiny T-shirts and dresses. And hats. I hope you like to wear hats, because I don't think there is anything sweeter to my eyes than a little girl in a flowered garden hat.

And honestly, after today, I have to say how happy I am that you are a girl. Not that I don't completely adore little Davie, but Nana was right: Boys are a handful! What a wonder his mind is, pulling him six hundred directions at once. He is starting to talk, and he spent the majority of the day running around the house and pointing at everything saying "Dis?"—

meaning "What's this?" I must have told him what the toilet was a hundred times. He also kept gently patting and rubbing my tummy, as if it were a most fragile kitten, and saying, "Baby . . . gentle, Davie . . . baby . . ."

But the funniest thing that happened all day was when I was standing in the kitchen, trying to make him a sandwich. I had an overwhelming attack of gas. I mean, I *farted*. Hugely. The sound exploded like an M-80 firecracker. Your daddy would have been proud. Bless his heart, Davie ran right up behind me, put his little sausage-patty hands against the back of my thighs, crouched, and looked up at my rear end, intrigued. "Hel-looooo?" he called to my butt. I guess he thought someone or something had tried to speak to him. I know Calista drops everything and runs into another room to avoid letting anyone other than me witness her fart, so perhaps he'd never heard a woman make a noise like that. Maybe he thought it was a foreign language. I just about passed out laughing. He giggled too, scrunching up his chubby face and clapping his hands together at his own joke. He just kept saying, "Hel-looooo . . . !" I haven't laughed like that since before your daddy died, little one. I was literally in hysterics, so much so that Julie heard me from her backyard and came over to make sure I was all right. When I told her what happened, she laughed almost harder than I had. It was so wonderful to let go like that. It was like being scrubbed clean on the inside of my skin.

After lunch I had the exquisite pleasure of giving Davie his bottle. He curved his solid frame around the basketball-swell of you and rested his head in the crook between my arm and left breast while he sucked deftly on his dessert of warmed milk. He reached up to play with my hair, twisting it around his stubby fingers as he looked deep into my eyes. And I know it sounds strange, but it felt as though he could read my thoughts with that intense gaze, as though he could feel my pain, my fears, and there he lay, comforting me with his huge, glassy cornflower-blue eyes. There is such a quality of wisdom in a child's eyes. I'm sure you will have it yourself. Gradually, though, those intuitive pools began to droop closed, as if invisible weights were added to his eyelids, one by one, until he could no longer manage to keep them open. I held him there, in the quiet cocoon of my lap, the entire time he napped, the warmth from his body melding into me, filling me with an unspeakably sweet serenity.

And now I am thinking that if I felt that much with him, a child who is not my own, I cannot even begin to imagine what having you in my arms will do to me. I think that maybe the love you have for your own child is a fiercer kind of love. I think it might be the kind of love that saves you.

A package arrived from Australia this morning. Knowing full well whom it was from, I let it sit on the kitchen table for most of the day, unopened. I kept having flashbacks of that ugly voodoo doll Mom sent me from Jamaica, so I think a small child-part of me was afraid to look inside. But late this afternoon curiosity finally got the better of me and I called Calista to come over so someone would be here when I opened it. She left Davie with Mike, who was home early from work, and arrived in under ten minutes.

I don't know exactly what I was imagining to be in the box, but it certainly wasn't what we found. Inside was a yellow crocheted throw, soft and fuzzy with age. The cotton edging was frayed and worn from use, with the names "Carol" and "Sarah" embroidered in the corners. When I lifted it to my face and inhaled its musty, ancient scent, a note fluttered to the ground.

Calista picked it up and read aloud: " 'This is the one thing I didn't throw away. Your Nana Cecille used it for me and later, I for you. I thought Calista might embroider whatever name you choose for the baby—she's handy like that, right?' " Calista set the note on the table and looked at me, her jaw dropped. "Wow" was her only comment.

"Isn't there a signature or anything?" I asked. She looked at the note again and said, "Nope, that's all she wrote. Wow. This is pretty thoughtful of the old bat. Totally out of character, of course, but still, really thoughtful." I smiled. "Yeah, well, you're right. It's pretty incredible. I don't quite believe it."

I hugged the blanket to me, the tears rising fast, and felt, for the first time since before my daddy left us, my mother's arms reaching out to hold me.

I have had the most gorgeous weekend. As a surprise, Julie booked an overnight stay at a local spa for Calista, her, and me. "Before you know it, the baby will be here and you won't have more than ten seconds to take care of yourself," she reasoned. "And I know that with a two-year-old, Calista doesn't even have that much time, and me, well"—she paused to shrug—"I just want to be spoiled. So I thought we'd give ourselves a much-deserved pampering extravaganza!" Both Calista and I were stunned by this gesture and offered to pay for our part of the bill, but Julie insisted the weekend was on her. "I had a good month, okay? My clients bought lots of goofy, expensive antiques. Let me do this." We tried, but there was no arguing with her.

The spa was actually a quaint bed-and-breakfast an hour or so north of Seattle. We were the only guests. A sturdy woman with strong-looking hands led us to our shared room, where at Julie's request, three twin beds had been moved in and made up with white eyelet sheets and goose-down comforters. "I thought separate rooms would be boring," she said. "Now we can talk all night."

The woman, whose name was Dory, smiled and said, "Your massages are scheduled with the staff in one hour. Feel free to use the hot tub out back beforehand. It helps to loosen your muscles." I told her that as I was pregnant, I couldn't sit in the hot tub—it wasn't good for me. "Hmmm . . ." she said. "Well, why don't you take a hot shower? Let it run as long as you like—we have an enormous water tank."

During my massage I lay on my side on a padded table, and that same strong-handed woman poured jasmine-scented oil over my skin. When Dory dug her powerful fingers into the knotted muscles in my lower back, I started to weep. I felt myself truly loosen for the first time in months, relaxing into the moment, and the tears just came, flowing gently down my cheeks. It felt as though they were leaking out of the deepest, darkest part of me; as if the hardest, most solid piece of my grief had begun to melt and these tears were quiet liquid evidence of something fractured beginning to heal.

Dory simply handed me a tissue and continued on with the massage. "Don't worry," she said softly, "lots of people cry. Even men. Body work brings up pain. Just let it out." And so I did. When she finished, I was vacant, drained. But something else had taken root in the empty places inside me; it felt like renewal.

The next morning, after all three of us had enjoyed facials, body wraps, and a glorious breakfast of fruit, cheese, and fresh-baked bread, Julie, Calista, and I curled in our beds for the hour before we had to check out. We whispered to one another about the pleasure of giving something to ourselves, when we, as women, are so used to only giving to others. "I feel guilty for letting someone else take care of me," Calista said, a note of sadness tingeing her voice. "Like I shouldn't be allowed. I had a really hard time keeping myself from offering to wash the breakfast dishes."

Julie nodded. "Yeah, but it's bullshit we feel that way. I say we do this at *least* twice a year to remind ourselves how wonderful we are. How much we deserve to be taken care of. If we don't know how to take care of ourselves, how can we possibly take care of anybody else? Am I right?" I smiled, slowly rolling from the bed, trying to maneuver the weight of my midsection so I wouldn't fall over. "Damn straight. And we're *not* going to make these beds, are we, Calista?"

Calista, who had already begun to pull up the sheets and arrange them neatly beneath the pillow where she had slept, paused, then curved her lips into a magnificent Cheshire grin. She yanked the bedding from the mattress, leaving it in a careless heap on the carpet. "Ta-dah!" she sang out loudly. Julie and I followed suit.

On the ride home the three of us were fairly silent, lost, I suppose, in our own thoughts. I know I thought hard about my desire to teach you, my little girl, to be a woman who knows her own needs: a woman who will stand up and say no to anything that compromises her sense of self; a woman who knows that she must take care of herself, first and foremost, if she desires to give anything of value to the people in her life. When I stayed with Nana, I remember her getting up every morning in the misty, glowing light of dawn and going down to the living room. I usually continued to sleep, but a few times I snuck behind her and watched from the top of the stairs as she lay spread-eagle in her flannel nightgown on the floor, taking huge deep breaths. I could see her stomach filling like a balloon, then deflating as she released the breath from her body. She would do that for at least ten minutes, stretching her chubby body this way and that, her breasts, free from any encumbrance, scooting toward her armpits like rabbits to their holes. Then she would sit in her favorite armchair and read from a slender leather-bound book, after which she would hug the book to her chest like a treasured child. The look on her face was one of soft, easy peace.

Once, over breakfast, I asked her just what it was she thought she was doing down there on the floor. She didn't seem surprised I had been watching. "I'm breathing, peaches," she said. "Just breathing. Your nana has learned she needs to take a moment for herself, every day." I nodded, hesitant, not sure exactly what she meant, then asked, "What do you read?" She smiled and brought me the book, a worn collection of poetry written by women. The pages were thin and some were crumpled, marked with prolonged, loving handling. I remember wishing I knew how to read big words like those; they looked so strong marching across the page. "All these beautiful words remind me of the glory of women," Nana said. "Of the magic we can create if we open our hearts. That's what I do down on the floor, Sarah. I'm making the decision to open my heart to every single one of my possibilities."

Before Julie and I stopped to drop Calista off at

her house, I told them this story of my nana, how she gave to herself first, every day. From the driver's seat of her Mustang, Julie raised an imaginary glass up to the darkening violet sky, urging Calista and me to join her. "To Nana," Julie said. "And to the magic of our infinite possibilities."

Julie was over at Calista's last night; since our spa weekend, the two of them have been spending more time together and have decided to plan a baby shower for me. I'm so happy they are getting along—their presence in my life is amazing. Calista has said it has been helpful for her to talk with Julie too. "I'm way more objective when she tells me what dealing with your husband's death is really like. I'm not so wrapped up in the situation. What she has to say about her experience makes me understand yours better, you know?" I thought I might be jealous of their becoming close—two's company, three's a crowd, and all that jazz, but strangely, I'm not. It just feels right, as though the three of us were meant to connect.

I spent last night alone, going back over much of what I've written to you, and I've realized that these letters have become a journal for me too. A place to set my feelings free. I also realized that you will probably not be ready to read much of this until you are an adult. And then it will be too late, because as you grow up, I want you to have something tangible to wrap your pudgy little fingers around, something you can open every day and use to get to know your daddy. Something that will remind you that he is here with us. That he helped make you.

So, I have decided on a project. This morning I made a huge pile of all of your daddy's letters, notes, and pictures and went to sit beneath the cool shelter of his tree. I sorted through them, pasting each in an enormous green scrapbook. Your scrapbook. I will fill this book with memories, memories you can touch and feel and ask me about. I have just over a month until you are here, and I promise to complete this task so that starting the day you are born I can introduce you to your father.

As I worked at cutting and pasting and writing in the margins of each page, tears dripped out of me as if I were a leaky faucet. But there was laughter too, a kind of fluttery, happy recollection of the circumstances that surrounded each memory I held in my hands. There is something wonderful about being able to smile again when I think of your daddy.

I also went through a stack of magazines, cutting out pictures of the foods he loved to eat, the sports he loved to watch, and the toys he still played with as a supposed grown-up man. I made collages of who he was so that if you ever want to know what his favorite dessert was, you can turn the page and see apple pie à la mode. You will never have to wonder if you look like him. You will know him as well as you know yourself. You will know the crinkles around his eyes, the slightly raised mole on his left cheek, the few stubborn, wiry black hairs that grew long in the space between his eyebrows, no matter how many times I plucked them for him. You will know the crooked bend of his mouth when he smiled, the wild twists of his hair when he first woke in the morning, the brilliance of his eyes, the muscle-man pose he struck every time a camera appeared. You will know the look of angelic peace that rested upon his face while he slept. You will know the chicken scratch of his handwriting and how it was in such utter contrast to the straight and beautiful lines of the buildings he designed. It always amazed me that a man who wrote so poorly could use a pen to make a living.

It surprised me a bit to find that I have pictures of him doing practically everything in our life together: eating, sleeping, dressing, shaving, taking showers, doing yard work. Many of the shots are mundane takes of daily activity that most people wouldn't consider worthy of capturing on film. I guess I've always thought that no matter how much we believe in our mind's ability to remember life's precious moments, solid, tangible evidence is a safer way to go. I wonder if I had some sort of premonition that I would need concrete proof of his life. If there was something mystical that urged me to document every moment I possibly could. I suppose I'll never know, but at least the memories are here for you. For you to know the man who was your daddy.

This morning, over cinnamon tea and currant scones, I worked up the courage to tell Julie about my suspicion of her having a part of my nana woven through her soul. "You have her voice," I said a bit nervously. We hadn't yet discussed our spiritual beliefs, and I wasn't quite sure what she'd think of my slightly modified reincarnation theory. But I trusted her not to judge me, so I plunged ahead. "And your voice isn't the only thing. You call my baby peaches. Nana used to call me that. And there's just . . . I don't know. Just something about you. I feel her presence when you're around. I've been thinking about her so much since Gavin died, wishing she were here to help me handle all this, I just feel like she might be reaching out to me through you, you know?"

After I spoke, Julie's eyes glossed with tears; she said it gave her chills to even think about it. "You're creeping me out," she said laughingly as she wiped beneath her eyes with the back of her hand. But I could see how touched she was by my words, and it made me even more sure that a spirit as beautiful as my nana's is given more than one chance to breathe in this world.

As I write this, I realize something else. Julie's coming into our life did more than give me comfort; it reminded me of magic. The kind of magic Nana lived and breathed, the kind of magic I want to pass on to you. From the moment you enter into this world, I want to do everything I know to share with you the gift of your Great-Nana Cecille. And it won't be enough to share her with mere stories, mere words. Words won't do a thing to capture the wonder of who she was. Instead, I will share her by telling you of fairies and their mystical dust and by burying those things that make you want to weep. I will share her by dancing with you in the grass on New Year's Eve and telling you you can fly, by lying next to you on the floor and teaching you to breathe in the glory of being a woman. Only then will you know her. More important, though, you will know what it is to believe in what you cannot always see. You'll know that when people seem lost to you, gone forever from this earth, you can still have faith. I promise, sweet girl, if you believe in those you love, they'll be there, right around the bend, ready to help catch you if you fall.

Both Julie and Calista went with me to my thirtieth-week checkup with Dr. Foster this afternoon. They sat in the waiting room, working out a menu for the shower. I told Dr. Foster how lucky I feel to have both of them in my life, helping me through this, and she encouraged me to definitely have them with me when I'm in labor. She thinks I'll need all the support I can get.

She prescribed even more twiggy cereal for the damn hemorrhoids I can't seem to get rid of, along with a daily dose of antacid for the heartburn that has been keeping me up at night. I've been trying to sleep propped upright by pillows, but my chest still feels as though someone is holding a blowtorch to my esophagus. We're up sixty pounds, if you can believe it. I've given up trying to fight it. My stomach is huge and my breasts are heavy and sore. The brush of my nipples against my bra is simply excruciating; I am naked as often as possible. Dr. Foster suggested that I try to expel the colostrum in my breasts by stimulating my nipples. I wanted to pretend I knew what colostrum was, but I didn't, so I asked, and she said it's a fluid, chock full of antibodies that fight infection, but if I release some of it, my breasts will start to feel better and I'll get some hands-on practice in breast-feeding technique.

In the car on the way home, I told Julie and Calista that it feels kind of sad for a woman to have to stimulate her own nipples. It's something your daddy would have loved about the whole pregnancy thing. "Oh, yeah," he would have said. "Mandatory nipple tickling . . . I like this pregnancy gig!" Julie cocked her head and adjusted the rearview mirror so she could look at me. "So, what are you saying? Are you asking for our help? One breast each?" I smiled, and Calista laughed. "I don't know, Sarah," she said. "I mean, I love you, sweetie, but not in that way."

When we got home, and Calista left to go pick up Davie from the sitter, I asked Julie if she would mind locating some good-sized boxes for me so that I can start going through your daddy's things and packing them up. I think that as I have been compiling your scrapbook, I've realized that it is time to try to put things in their proper place. I don't need his underwear in the drawer next to mine, or his sports equipment in the hall closet. And all his tools in the garage are simply taking up space. Someone else can use them, I'm sure. Maybe I'll donate them to some organization that teaches underprivileged men construction skills. Your father would have liked that. It is so much harder, I think, with all his things here, to believe that he's really gone.

Of course, I talked to him about it first. Sitting

under his fragrant, blossoming tree, I watched the emerald-eyed robin twitter and chirp above me as his mate used twine and twigs and mud to add the finishing touches to their nest. She is getting to be a chubby little thing . . . I wonder if she is pregnant too?

I waited for your daddy to appear, but when he didn't, I just started talking. I told him how seeing his possessions all around me only makes me hope for his return. I told him I needed to face the fact that this return is an impossible fantasy. My bottom lip quivered and my heart shook as I told him how much we missed him, but how we had to try to move on.

The warm spring air was still and quiet around me, hanging heavy like a damp blanket on a clothesline. I sat silent, listening for your daddy's response. His blessing, I suppose, his understanding of my need to put the physical reminders of his life into big brown boxes and store them away. After a few minutes passed, the male robin suddenly swooped down, right past my face—I swear I felt the whisper of his feathers across my cheek—and a breeze picked up around me, blowing my hair around my head in a confused cyclone. Petals shook loose from the branches above me and swirled like falling snow. No other trees or bushes swayed in this wind, and the chimes hanging from our back porch were mute. I took this as a sign that your daddy heard me and understood.

Now, for the hard part. The task of touching all his things, finding parts of him and our life together that I have forgotten, and filing them away. Kate thinks it will be a cleansing experience. Easy for her to say. I'm more apt to believe Julie, who says going through her husband's things was the hardest thing she did after Jimmy died. It was so final; like the tossing of a letter into the blue mailbox on the corner, there is no way to take it back. She discovered sections of him that she didn't know existed. His journal. His sex magazines. A bong and a substantial pile of moist, fragrant buds in a Ziploc bag. Hearing all this from her, I'm a little bit scared that I'll find out some things about your daddy that I won't like, things that will make me angry with him. But I can't keep my fear locked up. It will only make me explode.

I had another long conversation with Julie and Calista tonight. The three of us are practically inseparable, like adolescents in the throes of passionate new friendship, wanting sleep-overs and trips to the mall. Davie has been spending a lot of time home with Mike, who only shakes his head when Calista tells him yes, she is spending the evening with Julie and me. *Again.* The minute we get together, the words flow from our minds to our mouths without censure or hesitation. These women are my medicine.

Tonight we sat at our kitchen table, Julie twisting her fine straw hair around and around, biting off a split end here and there, while Calista sipped at a cup of tea. Julie said spending time with me had been bringing up a lot of stuff about how she felt when Jimmy died. "And you know what was the hardest part?" she asked. "The hardest part was when I started to think about all the bad times we had. It was as if I suddenly remembered that he wasn't a saint, that he wasn't always the perfect husband or friend or lover. That whole 'don't speak ill of the dead' routine really ran deep in me. I thought if I acknowledged his imperfections, I was somehow saying it was okay that he died. I was afraid I was dishonoring his memory, so I didn't allow myself to think about how he always forgot to call when he'd be late, or how he still sent Christmas cards to his high school girlfriend even though he knew it drove me crazy." She reached over to me, grabbed my hands in a vise grip, drove her gaze into me like a jackhammer, and continued. "Don't do it with Gavin. Remember his faults, okay? Honor them. They are part of who he was, and your little peaches, your baby, needs to know that her father wasn't perfect, or she will create unreachable standards for the men in her life. No one will ever measure up to her perfect, dead daddy." She paused. "Nor, for that matter, will any man measure up to your standards if all you do is moon over how incredible Gavin was. I know it's way too soon to even think about other men, and I'm still so sorry for hurting you by saying you'll know about what it's like to date, but you're young, Sarah. There'll be other men that will want to love you and your child. Make room for their faults. Make room for your own."

I swear, the wisdom that comes out of that woman. I never would have thought about telling you of the hard times, the adjustments to being married, the itch I sometimes felt to escape the commitment I had with your father and begin again without him. I barely let myself acknowledge that I ever even seriously considered scratching that itch. Your daddy and I married so young, and it was not even a year before I started having second thoughts about our decision. I had thought we were different, immune to the typical difficulties that plagued most couples. And it's true, we had good communication most of the time, but there were times I simply wanted to shoot him in the head. Not for any flagrant violation in particular, not because he ever hit me or yelled at me or drove himself between my legs despite my quiet cries of refusal. Gavin never inflicted anything even remotely resembling abuse. I think, instead, it was the cumulation of lesser transgressions, the tiny trespasses of thoughtless action that drove me to frustration with your daddy. His stinky gym socks on the kitchen counter, chubby, terry-cloth accordions tossed next to the fruit bowl. The piss drizzled on the toilet seat. The wet towel lumped on top of the goose-down comforter. The way he'd drink milk right out of the carton. The muddy footprints he slopped across the linoleum. His lack of consistent deodorant use. These were the crimes that offended me.

It's not that your daddy did these things intentionally, as if he knew they would bother me so he set out to make sure they happened. Not at all. Everything considered, he was a wonderful husband. He never forgot my birthday or our anniversary. For those special occasions he went to every florist in the city to find scarlet roses because he knew they are my favorite. He didn't laugh at me when I cried during long-distance phone company commercials. He kissed the inside of my elbow simply to hear the whimper of pleasure it sucked out of me. He put forth a grand effort to make me happy. It's just that every once in a while, I'd be looking at him seated across from me at our favorite restaurant or lying next to me in our bed, and I'd stare deep into his face, at his pointed nose and bushy black eyebrows and cavernous pores, and it was suddenly as if I were seeing him for the first time. And then the questions began to rise fierce within me, shooting off like bullets. Questions like: What in the hell am I doing here? Who is this person? Who have I become? What has happened to the life I was supposed to live?

When I had related most of this to Calista and Julie, Calista looked at me, her expression aghast. "That is *exactly* how I feel with Mike sometimes. You're telling me you felt this way about *Gavin*? About being married to *him*? But, he was so . . . I don't know. Romantic. Attentive."

"He also could be a pain in the ass," I said, acknowledging this for the first time since he died. The words felt strange in my mouth, but on some level I also felt relieved to have spoken them. Julie touched my hand in support, as if she knew the nature of the thoughts that were floating through my mind. I continued. "He was human, Calista. He did things that pissed me off. I just tried to focus on the good and accept the not-so-good. I always felt like you thought your problems with Mike would magically be solved if he were just more like Gavin."

She still looked surprised. "Well, I guess I did think it. You never told me any of this. . . ."

"Yes, I did. You just didn't listen. You saw all the romantic, mushy shit he did and you figured I was insane for complaining. You *told* me I was insane. So I stopped going into it with you."

"Sweetie," Calista said, "I'm sorry. I don't remember your trying to talk to me about it. I seriously thought it was just me who felt like my life wasn't measuring up."

An idea struck me. "Is that why you never wanted to talk with me about your problems with Mike?"

"Maybe . . ." she said thoughtfully. "Maybe I felt like you wouldn't understand since you and Gavin were so happy."

I felt sadness rise like a balloon up my spine. "We *were* happy . . . we just weren't as perfect as you thought. I think the only thing that made Gavin and me different from you and Mike was that we talked about everything—good or bad, big or small—as it happened. We were never afraid to talk about our feelings, you know?"

Calista nodded. "I know. Mike and I are terrible talkers. We're *loud* talkers, but we sure don't know how the hell to communicate. I've been thinking maybe—if he's willing—we should find a counselor. I don't know though. I feel kind of strange just picking a name out of the phone book, you know?"

"I could ask Kate for a referral," I said. "I'm sure she knows someone who's good with couples." I gave her a questioning glance.

She pressed her teeth into her bottom lip before she spoke. "Yeah. Okay. Might as well give it a try."

After talking about this more with Julie and Calista, I think we decided that most women experience these feelings at some time in their marriage—jagged, piercing feelings of "wait, I've made the wrong choices . . . please, let me start over!" Sometimes a woman just gets to asking herself why. She finds herself looking in the mirror and not recognizing who she sees. She is washing the breakfast dishes and stops in the middle of rinsing dried egg yolk off her blue-checkered stoneware and thinks, Is this it? Is this all I am? She thinks there should be more. I can't think of any other way to describe the way I felt. Such an intense longing, a reaching for that brass ring we all get told to strive for. Only we don't know what our brass ring is. What we do know is that it is out there somewhere, haunting us, dripping with the success that is meant to be ours. And then somehow we end up working at a job we aren't passionate about but are too terrified to quit; married to a man we love but who cannot truly understand the mystical wonder of us. And then a woman feels alone. So alone that she figures she would actually feel less alone if she were no longer married.

When these urges to leave your daddy snuck up on me, I'd take long, hot showers. I'd try to scrub my scalp hard enough to soak the shampoo into my brain and cleanse my thoughts. The kind of thoughts that said maybe I should just go ahead and bolt. I thought maybe I could go and live in a bamboo shack some-where down off the Gulf of Mexico, where I would gorge myself on mangoes and pineapple and sex. I would have a hard-bodied pool boy, Juan, who would hand-feed me juicy grapes and seduce me with a flick of his native tongue as we lay twisted together in the white-fire sand. I would dance naked in the brilliant midday heat, my body would become firm and dark with the rapture of my new life, and I would no longer worry about such irrelevant issues as bumpy thighs or sagging breasts or mole hairs or stretch marks. And then I'd think yes, that is the life I am meant to be living. Not here, not this, not with your father.

I'd stand there, contemplating my fate, clapping my palms flat against the tiles beneath the showerhead and watching the sudsy water spin down the drain. I felt weak, powerless, as though I were witnessing a life slip away. I wanted to know what had happened to my dreams. I wanted to know how it was that I was stuck already, only twenty-four years old and married, washing dishes and underwear and toilets instead of sailing around the world or backpacking through Europe or accepting my third consecutive award for best actress in a dramatic role. I wanted to know why I had not written the stories that were bubbling like hot tar within me, why I was not traveling the globe, healing people's hearts with words of hope for the future. I needed to know why I so easily sacrificed my opportunity for greatness and settled. For him. For your farting, food-mashing, butt-scratching father. And the answer always came back to this: Despite his sometimes intensely annoying idiosyncrasies, I simply could not imagine my life without him.

Of course, I am not without my own shortcomings. I'll probably regret writing this someday, someday when you read this and tell me, "See, Mom? Even you said you were bullheaded!" All right. I'll say it. I am. I am stubborn. I once argued with some nutrition major in college that milk not water was the most thirst-quenching natural substance. When she presented me with a journal article that proved me wrong, I still had to say, "Yes, but what does milk mostly consist of? Water!" I have an extraordinary need to be right. It pushes at every part of my life, and I have had to learn to rein it in when it begins to intrude on the health of a relationship. Whenever your daddy and I would disagree about something, he would shake his head and look at me with that hopeless I've-given-up-on-getting-you-to-understand expression on his face. Eventually I would have to concede on some topic in our discussion, even though secretly I still believed I was right. Which I usually was. But that is beside the point. I am sure there were times that your daddy looked at me and wondered what he was doing, if he had made the right choice in spending his life with me. It's human nature to question our decisions, whether it's healthy to do so or not.

I've come to believe that there are probably thousands of people with whom you could be happy for the rest of your life. I don't think it is a matter of finding "the" Mr. or Ms. Right and if you don't, you're screwed, destined to be alone forever. There are so many beautiful souls in this world, so many people you connect with along the path of your life, people that when you meet them, you feel as if your spirits must have waltzed together before they came to rest in your bodies. I believe it's a matter of with whom you choose to make the commitment. Your daddy got me a plaque one Valentine's Day that says "Commitment . . . I will go on choosing you." This says it in a nutshell, I think. Keep it in mind as you sit someday, pondering whether you should continue with a relationship. Question whether you are able to go on choosing that person in your life, everything he or she says and does and is—forever. And if I do the job I am supposed to in raising you, you will have the strength to say no if you need to.

The time is coming so close for you to arrive—only four weeks left with you inside me. I sat today, bloated and beached in the shiny walnut rocking chair Calista and Mike brought over last week, sliding my hands up and down over my swollen belly until my palms became numb to the sensation, tingling and detached from my arms. The gentle patter of rain against new spring leaves whispered of baby angels' feet.

I think I am gathering strength. I am breathing in whatever energy that comes from being silent, listening to the quiet messages of my spirit, messages that tell me I am stronger than I think, that I will endure, that I will be an amazing mother. Sitting there in your room, I closed my eyes and concentrated on your movement, feeling you swim and kick within me. Your dance brought my attention to an earthly wisdom, an understanding of something larger than myself at that moment, something universal that I think all mothers must experience. I felt part of some grand connection, a silver thread linking me with millions of other women, women who have given birth when their husbands were alive, dead or dying, at war, smoking cigars in the hospital waiting room, or holding their hand as a new life emerges from their bodies. These women are holding me up; they are holding both of us, my little one. I am not alone—I am surrounded by the tightly woven strength of those who have been here before me.

My elbows rested on the smooth arms of the chair, my hands spread out over my stomach, and I lifted my blouse up to feel the stretched and taut skin that contains you. I feel like a drum; if I tap at my stomach, the secret rhythm of life would echo out from inside me. My belly button pokes out only slightly now, somewhat humorously, like the tied end of a pale balloon, and I touched it lightly, feeling a twinge of pleasure as though I had somehow caressed your precious little cheek. This spot where I once was connected to my own mother, where her body fed me so I could grow, it is here that I am now fused to you. I suddenly felt more alive, more present at that instant than at any other I have ever experienced. Looking out the window, I was suddenly thankful. Thankful for this experience. I am beginning to realize Nana was right about yet another thing: how strong the hard times can make me, how much I can gain from them. Losing your daddy stripped me of my innocence, my naive, invincible nature, and opened my eyes to the wonder of pain, to the wisdom its lessons can bring.

This morning, while Julie and Calista decorated my living room for the afternoon's baby shower, I went out to lounge in the shade of your daddy's tree. I noticed my green-eyed bird's mate squatting protectively in her nest. The male robin, perched atop a nearby branch, was noisily chirping his song: "Cheer up cheer up!" He looked a little dangerous as he sang, with his fiery-red poofed-up chest, as though he would swoop down without hesitation, without mercy on anyone or anything that threatened his lady. She left only for a few minutes, probably to get some lunch, and it was then that I peeked inside the bundle of twigs and found that my suspicions had been accurate. Four small oval eggs, their smooth and glossy shells shining like large, pale sapphires, lay snugly in the base of the nest. I checked the encyclopedia and found out that their nestlings should hatch in about two weeks, about a week before your due date.

The shower was a success; Julie and Calista ended up inviting practically everyone who ever knew Gavin and me. The only thing that bothered me was how several guests wore carefully polite smiles, each looking as though someone had cut them out from a magazine and pasted them in our living room. It was terribly obvious how afraid they were of saying the wrong thing, as if mentioning your daddy's name would somehow break me. Five months ago, yes, I may have fallen apart at the seams. But now it feels as though my pain is beginning to melt into strength; my spine is a little straighter, my smile a little more true, and I want more than anything to speak of Gavin, to remember him with those who loved him along with me. I felt him all around us at the party; I felt him laughing with me at the roundabout way Mary Parker tried to find out if I was thinking about dating yet. I could almost see him, floating around everyone's cliquish conversations, sticking out his tongue at Mary, or, perhaps more likely, reaching out to comfort her unease.

Most of them brought wonderful gifts: beautiful butter-cream sleepers, diaper service for a year, black and white educational toys for newborns, and my personal favorite, a teddy bear the size of the greater metropolitan Seattle area. I stuck this huge black ball of cuddle next to your crib. I think we should call him Comfort Bear, but I'll leave that up to you. Julie must have spent a week in her kitchen preparing her gift of heat-and-serve meals: lasagna, tater tot casserole, clam chowder in a bag (which I'm dying to taste, to see if it is anywhere near as wonderful as my nana's recipe), French bread, waffles, pancakes—you name it, she cooked it, filling our chest freezer with enough food to last at least the first month of your life. What a relief it will be not having to think of such things, so that I can concentrate on being with you, spending my energies on learning to be your mother.

My God, how strange that sounds—me, your mother. I can't believe how close you are to being here. Three weeks, if all goes well. My body feels swollen, extended in directions I never thought possible. The lightest touch against my skin makes me want to cry out in a devilish cross between pleasure and pain, muscles twinge in my back and all around you. Dr. Foster and Calista say I am having Braxton-Hicks contractions, my uterus's dress rehearsal for your arrival. You have dropped into the lower part of my pelvis—"lightening" Dr. Foster called it. I can tell my stomach is hanging lower; you're not digging into my diaphragm anymore. I can almost breathe normally again. All at once I am terrified and thrilled and sad. I hadn't realized how accustomed I would become to having a life inside me. In fact, I am slightly disappointed to be coming to the end of the unmatchable intimacy that arises from housing an entire body within my own. I know the connection we will share when you leave my womb is precious in its own way, but I feel like I am saying good-bye to something felt between us that we won't be able to experience again, no matter how hard we try. The proverbial apron strings will begin to be cut the moment your first cry pulls the milk to my breasts.

I listened to stories from the women who came to the shower, tales of difficult births, two- to twenty-six-hour labors, the misty confusion that dusts the first days at home with your child. I cannot wait. All I want to do is sit and hold you, to stare deep into your ancient wisdom and learn everything we possibly can from each other. Of course I am frightened, but there is something within me now, a knowledge that I will be all right. Your daddy is watching over us, how can we not feel safe?

I have some good news for you: With two weeks to spare, it looks like I have chosen your name. Though perhaps I should say that your father suggested it to me and I fervently agree that it is the right and proper name for our daughter, the person whose life blossomed between us.

It was early this morning when Calista and I were in my bedroom, packing up the last of your father's clothes to be taken away to charity—except, of course, for his purple sweatshirt and a few other sundry outfits with which I cannot bear to part—when I came across a scrap of paper stuck between a couple of pairs of mismatched socks. It was a corner torn off a piece of yellow graph paper that he used to sketch out his design ideas; there was an edge of a penciled building on one side of the paper and on the back, just this: *Rose? Run past Sarah for okay. . . .*

Molasses tears flooded the muscles in my neck when I saw these words scratched across the page; I have to assume he meant this as a suggestion for your name, after my passion for the flower, after the memories we shared atop its petals. And right then I knew, I knew to call you Rose Cecille Strickland. I decided that after Julie's arrival in our lives, my nana's spirit was meant to be a part of your coming into this world, so the least I could do is honor her name by including it in your own. You are a lucky little girl, my Rose, to have two beautiful guardian angels watching over you in this life.

Calista saw my eyes well up and my fingers grasp the charm around my neck. She stopped folding the pile of clothes in front of her and asked, "What's wrong?" I pressed my lips together and shook my head, afraid I might really lose it if I tried to speak, but held out the paper for her to read. After doing so, she lifted her eyes to mine, chin trembling, and said, "Oh, Sarah. Oh, my god. This is fucking incredible. He's reaching out to you with this, don't you think? He wants you to know he's still here." My heartbeat still thudding in my ear, I nodded my agreement.

This afternoon I took the scrap of paper and glued it carefully onto the last page of your scrapbook, next to the final picture I took of your daddy, an image that captured him putting together your crib just a week before he died; his expression intent and determined, the tip of his tongue peeking out the edge of his mouth in a moment of serious concentration.

I feel ready now, so ready for you to arrive. I am cleaning furiously, picking up tiny dust balls in the tips of my fingers and carrying them all the way out to the garbage can in the alley. I feel the need for purity, for cleansing. I've been showering at least three times a day, scrubbing my skin until it shines with a luster that

I know comes more from your presence in my body than my diligence with a washrag. Julie saw me attempting to carry out the venetian blinds to the backyard and came over to scold me; she compromised by letting me at least spray them down before she hung them back up. I cannot help myself. It is an urge older and deeper than anything I have ever felt.

I keep checking on the robin's eggs, but they are still intact, their father standing guard while their mama focuses fiercely on keeping them warm. I hope they hatch before I go into labor. I want to know that they come out okay before you make your grand entrance. Hang in there, my little Rose, it's almost time.

The sun rose early this morning, spilling white shadows across my bed. I felt its warmth on my face and the pleasure that filled me was so vast, so expansive, I flung back the covers and let my naked skin be swathed in light, my midsection a mountainous silhouette stretching up the wall. Did you feel the heat melt into you? Was the light strong enough to penetrate the dark world to which you have grown so accustomed?

I rolled over to one side, extending my limbs as if a rope were pulling my ankles and wrists away from each other, and squealed with the relief that stretching brings. You twisted within me, and I think it was your foot that poked out at me, just under my left breast. I have to tell you, Rose, it is just about the strangest goddamn thing I've ever seen in my life. I was reminded of the scene in the first *Alien* movie, where the monster pops its way out of this character's stomach while the other crew members look on in horror. Wouldn't that be a first? I could just imagine the newscast: "Baby bursts from mother's belly, no delivery needed—film at eleven." I thought about calling Julie and having her come over to witness this happening, but then I remembered she was out of town for a few days on business. She made me promise not to go into labor before she gets back this afternoon. So far, so good. I've had a few contractions, but nothing severe enough to make me think it was time to get to the hospital.

When I finally managed the energy to excise myself from the bed, I waddled into the living room and saw that the light had followed me; a sort of spotlight rested over your daddy's ashes. The box shimmered, as if its surface were waving me over, beckoning me. And for the first time, I actually felt peace in handling this miniature coffin; I caressed it as though it were the finest porcelain, running my lips softly over its edges, whispering your daddy's name. Something washed over me—it felt strangely like your father's touch—and I knew that today I could bury him.

But first I had something to do. Now, I know when you read this, you will think that your mama suffered a bout of temporary insanity. Let me assure you that I was fully conscious of this decision, this final attempt to feel your father within me. Nothing about my actions was irrational, I knew what I was doing every step of the way. I set the kettle on to boil and selected the strongest-tasting herbal tea we had in the cupboard. The latch on your daddy's box was a bit sticky—I hadn't opened it in a while—so I jimmied it with a butter knife and then sat at the kitchen table, waiting. The box sat open in front of me, your father's ashes lying still, as if they understood the gravity of the moment. Outside, I heard the familiar chirp of the daddy robin, and then several whispering little peeps behind it, and I smiled; the nestlings had made it safely into this world. Then the sharp whistle of the kettle went off, and with a great deal of awkwardness (a characteristic that seems to accompany most of my movement lately), I pushed myself up and over to the stove, where I poured the boiling water into your daddy's MEAN PEOPLE SUCK BUT NICE PEOPLE SWALLOW mug. Bobbing the orange spice teabag beneath the surface, I carried the drink back to the table, and before I could change my mind, I scooped a small teaspoon of the finest powdered ashes from your father's remains and stirred them quickly into my drink.

My logic is this: Now there is a part of your father flowing in my blood, turbulent in my veins; my body will draw on whatever nutrients the ashes might contain—of course, I don't know if they contain any, but I will believe they do, and that is enough. I have taken your daddy into my body, where he will forever be a part of my physical being, the everyday functions of my flesh. He will pump through my heart with every breath I take. I felt a bit like a cannibal, but I pushed past the queasiness and into my determination to perform the ritual. I imagined it might be something my ancient female ancestors might have done to honor their dead husbands, and I felt strongly that I had done the right thing, even when my stomach softly protested as I sipped the hot, slightly grainy liquid down my throat.

I suppose I should have consulted Dr. Foster about the safety of doing this with you inside me, but honestly, I don't think it will do you any harm. It has been several hours and I feel fine. I hope you can feel your daddy flowing through you. My muscles feel tight around you, are you getting ready to appear?

After I dressed in your daddy's favorite sweatshirt and a pair of black stretch pants—the only outfit that can still accommodate me—I carried his ashes out to his tree. It was a gorgeous day, breezy sunshine swirled around us, sparse, cotton-sponge clouds marked the sky. It reminded me of our wedding day. Two perfect days to mark the beginning and end of our life together.

I peeked into the robin's nest; the nestlings' calcium prisons lay cracked and scattered about their reaching necks. Small, insistent chirps erupted from their throats, ceasing only when their mother dropped her mouth for them to gather nourishment. My heart filled up with joy at the sight. Four healthy baby birds, confident in their mother's ability to care for them, knowing instinctually that she will provide. The male bird perched at a distance, eyes darting around, searching for unseen enemies. I thought about how this could be your daddy, my sweet Rose. How this little bird family is a shadow of our existence. Sometimes the universe reaches out to speak to you in the strangest manner. We have to keep reminding ourselves to listen, or our lessons just might pass us by.

The earth was soft and moist between the knotty roots of the tree; I used no tools, digging determinedly with my fingers to loosen the ground. Black half-moons emerged beneath my nails. I took an enormous breath, filling my lungs to their capacity and slightly beyond, then held your daddy's ashes up to the sky. "I know you're here, Gavin," I said. "I know you always will be. You'll grow into the life of this tree, nourishing it as you have nourished me and our daughter. I feel you, baby . . . I feel you all the time. I know it's time to let you go."

The box flipped upside down, spilling his ashes over. I worked him into the ground, mixing his soul and his humor and his love into the soil. Tears ran down my face, racing off the tip of my nose, and yet I labored to smile, to laugh a little, to honor your daddy. To think of every wonderful moment we ever spent in each other's arms. To remember the joy he brought into my life, the loosening of my spirit, the freeing of my fears, the confirmation of my worth. I fought the urge to stop, to bring him back inside our home, as if having his ashes within those four walls would somehow make him more alive. But he is alive, Rose. He is wrapping himself around us, cocooning and protecting us. I dug in deep, stirring and working and mixing until there was no trace of bone, only the dark, rich dirt, fluffy and new. A fertile surface, a fresh beginning. I felt peaceful, sure I had done well, a beautiful and true burial for the man I will love for the rest of my life.

I slid this day into a tiny box within my mind, a safe and quiet resting place. A box I can open and remember whenever I need calming, whenever I need peace. I am ready now, Rose. I am ready for our life.

You woke me just moments ago. Sharp twinges in my lower back, quickening aches rippling through my belly. I stood and dug my fingers into the muscles just above my butt, trying to alleviate the constrictions. It's starting, isn't it? You are coming. I buried your father only yesterday, and now you are on your way, an entire week before you are due.

Part of me wants to scream stop, wait, I thought I was ready, but I'm not. I'm not ready to be a mother. Good God, I'm about to have an entire human body pass through an opening the size of a fifty-cent piece. Jesus, this is going to hurt. I'm scared. What if I can't do this? I know Calista and Julie will be there for me, holding my hands, urging me on. I know I can have an epidural if I want to, if the pain gets to be too much. But I've worked so hard, learning to focus on my breathing, to believe that my body knows how to bring you into the world. I want to feel every sensation, trusting my body's instincts to carry me through the pain . . . oh . . . hold on. There's another one. Shit. I forgot I'm supposed to be keeping track of how far apart the contractions are. What has it been since the last one—twenty minutes? Are you keeping track? Is this as terrifying for you as it is for me? Do you wonder what the hell is going on? Gavin, where are you? Do you know what is happening? Do you realize your daughter is about to be born?

I just called Julie and Calista; they are both on their way over. I'm pretty sure I've got a few hours before I need to get to the hospital. My water hasn't broken and it has definitely been at least twenty minutes since the last contraction. I've got a bag by the door filled with your newborn sleepers and T-shirts, unbelievably tiny diapers, the blanket your grandmother sent, and a picture of your daddy. It's four o'clock in the morning and I am absolutely ravenous, but I'm not supposed to eat or drink during labor. I'm probably going to go to the bathroom all over the hospital table once I start pushing anyway; Dr. Foster says that it's pretty common. My god, what a raw experience. Completely primal: screaming, shitting, pissing, crying, writhing, then joy. Pretty much the whole gamut of life experience rolled into a few hours. Once again I'm having a hard time choosing between elation and terror.

I keep getting up from this writing and walking around our house, touching the walls, the lamps, the furniture, thinking how this home will never be completely empty again. This place will become our life together, full of laughter and tears and frustration and pain and anger. But it will be full. Oooh, there's another one. I gotta pee like a racehorse.

It has been five hours since this all began, and the pain is coming a little quicker now, starting at the top of my belly and working down toward my hips. Are you okay, Rose? Can you breathe all right? I'm terrified of the umbilical cord wrapping around your neck and choking life right out of you before you've even had the chance to live.

Julie and Calista are here, clucking around me like mother hens, rubbing my back, leading me around the house when a contraction hits. It's not hurting as much as I feared it would, although the worst may be yet to come.

I always thought that when my water broke it would be a flood. I pictured a river of fluid gushing down my legs, the floor awash by a small lake. It really wasn't much at all. Although there was this pinkish, gelatinous-looking blob lying in the middle of the mess on the bathroom floor. I think it was the mucus plug. (Is there anything more disgusting than those two words placed together?)

We're leaving for the hospital now, Rose. My contractions are only eight minutes apart—we are moving headlong into the active phase of labor. The next time I write, I will have touched your tender skin, smelled your sweet baby smell, felt your lips to my breast. Hold on. It may be a bumpy ride.

Oh god baby, you aren't here. We've been at the Childbirth Center for an hour and they can't find your heartbeat. Four nurses have looked for it and failed. Dr. Foster isn't here yet. Jesus, oh god, don't be dead. Please oh please, my sweet girl. I feel movement inside me, but I can't tell if it's you or just a contraction trying to expel a dead baby. They're coming every six minutes, but we're not making any progress and I'm already exhausted. Dammit. I can't let this happen. You have to be all right. I've seen you move beneath my skin. Where did you go, Rose? Please, don't do this to me. After everything we've been through, please, please, don't leave me too. I could not survive. There would be no reason to live.

Calista and Julie are doing their best to convince me that everything is fine, but I can see the fear hovering in the corner of their eyes. Their smiles are sharp and false, as if fishhooks are dragging up the corners of their mouths. They're thinking, *What are we going to do with Sarah if her baby is dead?* Good fucking question.

Nobody can believe that I am lying here, writing in the middle of all this, but it is the only thing that is keeping me sane.

Both Julie and Calista went outside my room a moment ago, to the nurses' desk, breathing down those poor women's necks, yelling at them to get their shit together and find your heartbeat. I heard Calista's low, insistent tone. "Get the fuck in there. No, not in a minute. Now. Do you hear me?" I can see the nurses looking at me through the glass partition, their expressions pretending to be reassuring. They're scared too.

They can't find Dr. Foster. Julie has gone over to the hospital answering service to stand over the operator as Dr. Foster is paged so she can be the first to talk with her. Calista is with me, pacing in and out of the room to alternately check on me and scream at the nurses. My heart is thick with fear. I jump at every movement inside me, straining to locate where it came from. My blood pressure is rising, and the contractions keep coming. I am refusing to believe you are dead. God, I'm scared. Julie isn't back yet; Dr. Foster must have her pager off. Calista is out at the nurses' desk again, her fists clenched at her sides.

A fifth nurse finally just came into my room, an older woman, one I hadn't seen yet, looking a little frightened of Calista, who stomped in behind her. The nurse placed a stethoscope all over my belly, then reached up inside me. "Ohhh . . ." she said as she pulled back her gloved hand. "Sarah? Who is your doctor?" Julie walked through the door and answered for me. "Dr. Foster. I just talked with her. Her car broke down on the 520 bridge, but she's on her way.

What the hell is going on?" The nurse pursed her lips but said nothing and walked quickly out of the room. Calista exploded. "Goddammit! What does it take to get a straight answer in this place?"

Both she and Julie ran after the nurse, and now you and I are here alone, Rose. Waiting. I'm writing between the mind-numbing spasms that grip all around you. It's probably going to be impossible to read any of this—the words are all over the page—but I feel the need to document every moment I can before the pain gets to be too much. I don't know what else to do. Oh god, what if I killed you with my grief? What if you are dead and everything I've been going through has been pointless? Gavin, can you hear me? Please, oh, please, baby. We need you here with us.

I am holding my breath, trying to feel your heartbeat. I know it's in there somewhere. I have to believe it. I can't believe anything else.

After seven hours of first-stage labor, Dr. Foster finally made it in to see us, Rose. They had such a hard time finding your heartbeat because no one thought to put the stethoscope against my back. That last nurse figured it out when she stuck her hand up inside me and felt the top of your head instead of the back of it. When you moved down into my pelvis, you decided to twist around and enter the world faceup instead of tucking your chin into your chest. Dr. Foster told me I could still deliver you naturally if the distance across the top of your skull wasn't too wide to fit through my pelvic bones.

As limp and tired as I was, I cried thankfully that you were still alive. At the same time, I was bone-shakingly terrified I wouldn't be able to get you out. Dr. Foster said a cesarean was a possibility, but she would do everything possible to avoid the procedure. "I've delivered plenty of facial presentations, Sarah. Your labor may take a little longer," she warned, "but as long as she fits through and there's not too much pressure on her face, it's perfectly safe, I promise."

We hit transition about two hours after seeing Dr. Foster. My cervix was at nine and a half centimeters—not enough to push. My *god*, Rose, how I wanted to push. As soon as a nurse verified I was fully effaced and dilated, Dr. Foster arrived and assured me that feeling your tiny head, she had determined it was small enough to pass through my pelvis. "She's a dainty girl," she said, smiling. She asked one of the nurses to dim the overhead lights, directing the only bright lamp in the room to focus between my legs. The soft background sound of water whispering over smooth stones in a brook filled the air around us. I remembered Dr. Foster had done the same thing with lights and music during Davie's birth, believing a peaceful environment is inherently necessary for a child's smooth transition from the womb to the world.

Julie and Calista stood on either side of me, encouraging me to keep breathing through every body-ripping contraction, then propping me up and helping me adjust into any position that managed to even slightly relieve the pain of pushing. I first tried lying on my side, knees apart and bent up to my chest, but after an hour of pushing and not making much progress, I ended up on my knees at the head of the bed, hands slapped up flat against the wall. Calista and Julie climbed in front of me and used all their strength to hold my upper body vertical, since Dr. Foster suggested that gravity often lends a hand in this process.

Jesus, it hurt. Don't let anyone ever tell you labor is just like cramps. Compared to what I went through today, cramps are a fucking picnic. I wept between contractions, terrified that despite Dr. Foster's assurance that you would be fine, you would emerge from me blue and still, strangled by my sorrow. Toward the end, after another bout of intense pushing and two-minute-long contractions, I wildly shook my sweat-drenched head, insisting, "I can't do this . . . oh god, I can't. I'm so tired. I can't get her out. Just get her out of me."

"She's almost here, Sarah," Calista said. "Hold on. Just hold on." Julie sniffed hard, pushed my hair back from my face, and smiled at me. "Keep breathing, okay, sweetie? They're almost done, I promise. We love you. Everything is going to be just fine."

"Just a couple more pushes, Sarah," Dr. Foster encouraged. "I can feel her shoulders. . . . I just have to turn them a little to pass through your pelvis. I know you can do this . . . *you* know you can do this. Come on, one more push, okay?"

It was then I turned my eyes to the window and saw your daddy standing there, leaning toward us. His voice was suddenly inside my head, telling me that I could do this, I could make it through. I felt him holding me up from across the room, urging me to believe, to grasp onto hope and not let go when I heard your cry soar through the air on angels' wings. A tidal wave of relief crashed through me, and I suddenly knew that every ounce of pain I've gone through since your daddy died, every doubt and fear and insecurity I've experienced, was for this moment, this pure knowledge, this absolute certainty that I was put on the planet to be your mother. When I looked back to the window, your daddy was gone, but my heart was too full to feel any sadness. I had no room for sorrow or regret or pain because you, my child, my sweet, sweet Rose, you were here. We were together.

Calista brought Mike and Davie in a while ago to meet you, but they stayed only a minute, since I asked to be alone with you. Julie was here too, but I think she is busy now, chatting with a cute physician's assistant she met in the cafeteria. "His name is Jason," she said. "He's six years younger than me and he still wants to go out!" I smiled hazily in response, shooing her off with a wave of my hand.

It is late now, and you are sleeping as I write this, lying serenely on your back in the bassinet beside me, wrapped in the soft blanket that held both me and your grandmother on the days we entered this world. Your tiny pink starfish hands are curled softly upon your chest. You are perfect. When you first emerged from me, your poor face was swollen and red, puffed and angry from the pressure it endured in my womb, but the swelling is already starting to go down, and every piece of you is in the designated spot. Your wise eyes are a brilliant shade of turquoise, a sure sign, the maternity nurse assured me, that they will eventually match your daddy's green. I cannot believe the amount of black fluff upon your head, a silky mess of dander standing straight up, as though a clumsy electrician came along in my womb and stuck your finger in a light socket. Your mouth, red and moist as a lilliputian strawberry, works away, puckering soundlessly for my breast, and soon the nurse will be here to help me try to feed you again. My breasts are rocks, solid and pulsing, leaking in anticipation of fulfilling their purpose. You weren't hungry when they first placed you against me. You closed your mouth and seemed to want to sleep, to recover from the arduous journey of entering this world. Dr. Foster says this is completely normal and I shouldn't worry. So I'm trying not to. But honestly? There suddenly isn't enough worry in my brain. I am worrying about everything: about nuclear war and the widening gap in the ozone layer; about yellow dye number five and plane crashes and objects in our house small enough for you to choke on. You are so beautiful . . . so vulnerable. A primitive urge to protect you is screaming through me. I think of the horror I felt in losing your daddy—the mind-bending, soul-racking grief that spread like a stain in my life, obliterating everything in its path; how I thought his death would be the end, and it makes me desperate to weave a silken web of contentment around you, filling your life only with what is beautiful and true.

Of course, if I've learned anything in the past six months, I've learned that what is true is not always beautiful. In a single blow, the truth of your daddy's death crumbled everything I had thought would last forever. But with you lying here now, it dawns on me that what I felt was the end was really only a threshold. I have traveled through the passageway of grief and the journey has made me see the world through newborn eyes, eyes that view every person as a gift, every breath as a blessing, every loss as an opportunity to grow.

I hope you know this, Rose, as life opens up before you now, granting your soul its lessons to learn; I hope you know that there are no endings. There are only those chances to begin again.

ABOUT THE AUTHOR

AMY YURK lives in Bellingham, Washington, with her husband. This is her first novel.